Steinhof

Also by Carola Hansson:

The Dreamt Child
Andrej
A Complaisant Man

Steinhof

Carola Hansson
translated by Irene Scobbie

ARCADIA BOOKS
LONDON

Arcadia Books Ltd.
15–16 Nassau Street
London W1W 7AB

www.arcadiabooks.co.uk

First published in the United Kingdom 2002
Original Swedish edition published by Norstedts Forlag AB, Stockholm
Copyright © Carola Hansson, 1998
Translation copyright © Irene Scobbie 2002

A catalogue record for this book is available from the British Library

ISBN 1-900850-66-4

Typeset in Ehrhardt
by Northern Phototypesetting Co. Ltd, Bolton
Printed in the United Kingdom by Bell & Bain Ltd, Glasgow

Arcadia Books Ltd acknowledges the financial support of The Arts Council of England,
London Arts, the Swedish Institute, Stockholm and the Anglo-Swedish Foundation,
London.

Arcadia Books distributors are as follows:

in the UK and elsewhere in Europe:
Turnaround Publisher Services
Unit 3, Olympia Trading Estate
Coburg Road
London N22 6TZ

in the US and Canada:
Consortium Book Sales and Distribution
1045 Westgate Drive
St Paul, MN 55114-1065

in Australia:
Tower Books
PO Box 213
Brookvale NSW 2100

in New Zealand:
Addenda
Box 78224
Grey Lynn
Auckland

1956–7

1

Later, when Magda had already described the escape so often that the event had petrified into a kind of final form, it was always the sudden appearance of the boy that she would consider the decisive factor, always that afternoon, 27 October, she would emphasize: that was the turning point in her life. Perhaps because it really was. Or perhaps because half-subconsciously she had chosen it – quite simply – because there in Traiskirchen she needed something firm and stable to hold on to when everything seemed on the point of disintegrating and disappearing.

Of the almost one hundred pupils at the school only thirteen had been left living there (for the more superstitious or imaginative of her listeners she used to emphasize the exact figure very particularly) – thirteen little girls who naturally ought to have left long ago too, but whose parents neither she, Dóra nor Maria had managed to track down, even though, when the boy appeared, the revolution was already into its fifth day.

"The twenty-seventh," she would always underline, as if of the greatest importance, "the twenty-seventh was a Saturday".

It had just started to grow dark.

And it was here – even before she'd noticed the strange boy – when she was on the point of going out into the courtyard to fetch some water but instead had remained standing on the threshold, that she was suddenly overcome (even though she

had seen this picture thousands of times), genuinely struck by
the beauty of it: the rounded courtyard like a pale shell, the
black forest all around, the dark-blue sky with its single
brightly shining star over the shed roof, and the specific lighting, the almost artificial twilight which seemed to rise up out of
the ground, and which made the leaves of the virginia creeper
stand out with such an intense dark-red glow – it was here, it
seemed to her, at just this moment, that everything had its
beginning.

When the silence was so profound that it made her feel
slightly giddy.

When not a leaf stirred and even the fat grey pigeons at the
edge of the well seemed to have turned to stone in the middle of
a movement.

Such tranquillity! Perhaps that was what she was really
thinking – at the very moment that a window on the first floor
was thrown open and the girls' voices penetrated down into the
courtyard. Such a strange tranquillity! Then she shivered, suddenly aware of the unusual cold, pulled her cardigan more
tightly around her and hurried off across the courtyard. When
she was halfway across she heard the window being closed again
behind her. The voices disappeared and it was as quiet as before.
At the well she shooed away the pigeons, placed the bucket on
the edge and bent forward to reach the rope which was tied to
the top of the hoist.

It was then that she caught sight of him.

It was then, just as her fingertips touched the coarse knot in
the rope, that she realized that someone was standing there outside the gate; a young man or a boy – she couldn't immediately
decide his age. She was only aware of his presence, that he was
standing there, silent and vigilant, and that, tensely watchful, he
was following her slightest movement.

She felt slightly uneasy.

How long has he been standing there? she wondered.

And what does he want?

She hesitated. Just then little Erzsébet came running across the courtyard, the girl's eyes shining eagerly and in her outstretched hand holding something that she obviously had to show – a rather worn blue ball with white spots. When at the next moment Erzsébet threw her arms around Magda's waist, Magda bent down to her and before the girl had had time to say anything, whispered that she should hurry back indoors to Dóra and wait for her there. Erzsébet looked at her in amazement and then obeyed without a word. Magda remained beside the well until she saw the school door close again. Then she turned and started to walk towards the gate.

She walked slowly, her heart beating fast: the strange figure really frightened her. And yet for some curious reason she was also afraid that he would disappear – disappear as suddenly and surprisingly as he had appeared. When she got closer she saw that he was smaller and slighter than she had thought, surely no more than twelve or thirteen years of age. When she got even closer she noticed that despite the cold he had no outdoor clothes, his shirt was torn, his whole body was shivering and he was very dirty. It wasn't until she had got right up to the gate, however, that she discovered that he was carrying something on his back – something that seemed to be very heavy.

A child! she thought in amazement.

It was indeed a child he was carrying: a little boy whose head was hanging down as if he were asleep. Asleep or pretending to be asleep.

She watched them both silently for a moment.

"What do you want?" she then asked.

The boy stiffened, crouched down a little and then backed away a few paces.

Then she was ashamed. It's all these rumours, she thought. All these horrible, contradictory rumours.

She opened the gate. "Come in," she said.

5

"Don't be frightened," she added when she saw him hesitate, then she stretched out her hand (this time he didn't back away), took him across the courtyard, through the school door, up the hall stairs, past the row of closed classroom doors and out into the kitchen, where dinner had just been prepared: there was a smell of boiled cabbage, and through the open door to the dining-room she could see Maria guiding the thirteen girls to their places at the long table beside the window. Dóra was busy slicing bread. When she caught sight of the strange boy she was startled. When at the next moment she caught sight of the child on his back she put down the knife and hurried to close the dining-room door. Then she went up to the boy, lifted down the child (it really was asleep) without a word, carried it over to the stove, made it comfortable on the pile of washing, and finally spread a cardigan over it before returning, still silent, to the table and continuing with her interrupted work.

Magda placed the boy at the other end of the table. She took a bowl out of the cupboard, filled it to the brim with soup and put it in front of him, along with a spoon, a thick slice of black bread and a dish of paprika. Then she sat down opposite him. She observed how he hesitated at first and then after a shy look at Dóra fell on the food and began to eat hungrily and without lifting his eyes from the bowl for a moment.

"What do they call you?" she asked.

When he didn't reply she filled a glass of water and pushed it towards him. Then she continued to observe him silently for some time, before finally leaning over the table. "You really must tell me what you're called," she whispered. "And where you come from."

He went on stubbornly staring down at the soup bowl, however. He just ate more slowly than before, stirred his soup slightly each time before lifting the spoon cautiously to his mouth. And when, despite his dismissive attitude, she continued to question him, she still didn't find out very much.

Admittedly he did gradually respond, but reluctantly, and in monosyllables – she thought that he was still frightened and didn't really trust them. Often he began a sentence and then broke off after only a few words. There was something about a market place (he still wouldn't name the town) and about a huge crowd. About people singing.

"They were all singing," he muttered. "All the people in the market place were singing."

Here he fell silent. His face grew even paler than before, and now he refused to say anything more. When she asked how long he'd been running away he merely shrugged his shoulders; when she wondered where he was actually on his way to he gave her a quick, hateful look before turning away.

After a pause as long as eternity she handed him an apple.

To her surprise he actually accepted it, grabbed it with hungry fingers and with a kind of suppressed anger, for a fleeting moment before he sank his teeth into it, it even looked as if he was smiling: his eyes did indeed shine, as if the taste of the apple had aroused a memory of a time so endlessly remote that it seemed to belong to another life. And suddenly the words poured out of him: in a slightly shrill voice, and stumbling over his sentences, he began to describe in detail life at school, at the new red-brick school in the centre of town where he had started only two months ago. He related this in a muddled, disjointed way and, so it seemed to her, really mostly for himself, and yet there was an intensity in his voice which made the particulars of his story stand out with almost hallucinatory clarity. He described the lessons, the food parcels and the shaded school-yard, the stale smell of warm milk and the croaking of frogs at dusk. He devoted a long time to the football matches in the park nearby and even longer to an excursion to Fertö Tava, where what obviously had made a special impression on him were the tall reeds, a flat-bottomed boat and a strange bird with red pointed wings, whose name even the teacher didn't know.

Mostly, however, he talked about his mates. There was some-body called György who had a white dog, there was László, Pal and József. "Real mates," he smiled.

He stopped abruptly, looked at her, newly awake, with the empty gaze of someone who has just woken from a dream. He then stroked his hand over his hair.

"We made bombs," he said contemplatively, "petrol bombs. Bottles with petrol that we threw at the Russian tanks."

There was something hesitant about his voice, almost friendly. It was mostly those four, he said, György, László, Jószef and himself. It hadn't been difficult at all. They had learnt at school how to make bombs like that, the actual process.

In gym lessons in the third form.

All the boys in his class were good shots as well.

He twisted and turned the half-eaten apple.

The secret was the actual spin, he explained, to be able to spin with the wrist at just the right moment. And a few days ago, early one morning, they had – though not György, because he was ill, and not Jószef because he had to take a message for his mother, but László and himself – they had managed a few real bull's eyes this time at a Russian armoured car: the bombs had flown straight through an open window. There had been an enormous bang and the Russian soldiers had died on the spot.

"All of them. They burned up. We stood there and saw them burn."

He said it just like that, abstractedly, with dried apple juice at the corner of his mouth.

"Three burning corpses in the back seat and two in the front."

There was silence.

She moved as if to get up. She wanted more than anything to say something, anything, not perhaps something comforting, anything like that would have been impossible (any attempt at comfort would have been like insulting him or, even worse, to comfort him would in the most terrible way have implied an acknowledgement of what he had said, a kind of sanction and judgement), no, she wanted to say something quite different, something which would at a stroke expunge what he had just described, something which would erase his words from their inner blackboard – or at least make it impossible for him to utter another word.

But she said nothing.

She looked at him in silence.

And he continued. Just as she had feared, some more words followed, although barely audibly – something about a woman with her head shot to pieces, about a bag of sweets and about the night that he and his brother had spent in the forest.

Only then did he finally fall silent.

Then everything happened very quickly.

He lowered his arm, the apple fell from his hand and while she gazed, as if transfixed, at the core embedded in the white flesh of the apple, at the spots on the peel and on the small, remarkably even, indentations from his teeth, he yawned, sighed and with a light thud fell over the table where he remained lying as if unconscious, with his arms hanging by his sides and his head resting against the edge of the soup bowl.

She made up a bed for the children on a mattress in her own room. In their sleep they inched close to each other, the little boy soon lying with his head on his brother's shoulder and an arm around his waist. She herself had difficulty going to sleep. While she lay awake staring out into the darkness, she wondered what would happen now – to both the strange boys and to the girls, these thirteen girls who still remained at the school. What will happen, she wondered, if the situation gets worse? And if the food gives out? And how can Sándor be so optimistic and so sure that we'll finally win? It struck her suddenly that the strange boy had never actually said what he was called. That they didn't know the name of either him or his little brother.

I simply must get him to tell me his name, she thought.

Immediately afterwards she fell into a heavy, drug-like sleep which lasted right until morning.

When she awoke the boy had gone.

His little brother, on the other hand, was still there.

She sat in her room the whole morning with the child in her lap. She sat on a chair by the window and he clung to her like a little baby monkey, sweaty, tense and with his head burrowed in her armpit. She supposed he must be hungry, but when she asked if he would like something to eat he only crouched down even further; sometimes a low whimpering passed his lips. Dóra and Maria had to take care of the girls: they took morning assembly, served breakfast and took them on their customary Sunday walk to Maria Magdalena church (afterwards [she just found it so amazing:] nothing, not even the violent disturbances, could prevent Dóra from taking the girls to Mass).

The sun rose slowly over the tree tops.

The shadows shortened.

After two hours the girls returned from church. At the sound of their excited voices from the courtyard she quickly rose from her place near the window and carried the boy downstairs, out into the kitchen. After a lot of coaxing she managed to get a little food down him: a few spoonfuls of porridge, a warm maize bun and half a mug of milk. A short while later he fell asleep in her lap. Then she wrapped him in a blanket and sat down with him on the bench beside the well. The sun warmed them. She observed him while he slept. What age could he be? she wondered. Four? Five, perhaps. Only now did she notice that he had unusually high cheekbones and large, rather shiny, jug ears. She thought he reminded her of someone. Only she couldn't think who.

Soon after that he awoke.

10

Their eyes met very briefly before he looked down again. She stroked his coarse, short hair. Then she pointed out over the courtyard.

"Look how the virginia creeper's gleaming in the sun," she said, "and how blue the sky is over the forest." She drew his attention to the girls, too, playing hopscotch in the shade of the walnut tree.

"The girl with dark hair is called Agnes," she said. "The one with glasses is Zsofi. And the smallest one, the little tubby one who's just thrown the stone, is called Erzsébet."

He was silent.

Erzsébet jumped. One square. Two. At the third she did a half turn, caught sight of them and stood motionless with one foot in the air (just that detail would later be etched in her mind: Erzsébet's thick grey stocking concertina-ing round her ankle and her brown boot with its loose laces dangling) – until the other girls too turned round and, as if on a given signal, all came rushing together towards them across the yard.

Only a few yards from the bench they stopped. Stood there in a semi-circle in front of her, silent, looking inscrutably at the boy in her lap. Until Erzsébet suddenly stretched out her hand and touched his hair lightly.

"What's he called?" she murmured. "And what's he doing here?"

Magda hesitated. But before she had time to say anything the girls had turned tail again (perhaps they didn't really want to know anything?), rushed off towards Maria who was just coming through the gate with a bucket of onions, and began to shower her with requests for an excursion, a real Sunday excursion up into the mountains – such as had been promised as long ago as last summer but which had never materialized. They said there was sure to be lots of mushrooms in the forest and perhaps with a little luck they would find some cranberries that hadn't been spoilt by the frost.

11

Maria smiled. "Not today," she said. "But soon. Perhaps next Sunday even."

The girls soon returned to their game under the walnut tree. Magda looked at the boy.

He was asleep again, with his mouth half open, his forehead perspiring. When in his sleep he turned his head she suddenly noticed – a discovery which filled her with unexpected tenderness – that his face was remarkably asymmetrical and that his left ear actually stuck out more than the right one.

Sándor rang already early on Monday morning to ask why she hadn't come to town on Sunday as promised. While she silently examined her conscience and realized to her dismay that she had quite simply forgotten about their meeting, she told him, although in fact (she didn't really know why herself) she didn't want to mention it, about the boy's sudden appearance and his equally sudden disappearance and about the little boy who had remained behind.

"He's no more than a few years old, perhaps four," she said.

And in the same breath she assured him that she had tried several times on Sunday afternoon to ring Sopron, both the café at Fö tér and the flower shop in Scent Mihály utca (perhaps, she was to think later, she really had done so), and that she was sorry about what had happened (something that was in any event quite true: she could have wept with the disappointment).

"He's perhaps four," she repeated, "and he hasn't said a word. Not even his name." Sándor laughed.

"You wouldn't have been able to get hold of me anyway," he said.

It transpired that he hadn't been at home either in the afternoon or in the evening. After waiting in vain for her for over an hour at Fö tér he had gone off to a meeting at the university: they had set up a revolutionary council among the students, he said, and he himself had been appointed leader of the health care group.

He sounded happy and very enthusiastic.

An enthusiasm that over the following week – for she was to talk to him on the phone more often these days than ever before – seemed to grow stronger by the hour: "Victory", he already declared at an early stage "isn't just something discerned in the distance: it's already here." On Tuesday he told her that even the border guards had now gone over to the revolutionaries' side and that for a bag of flour or potatoes they'd let anybody cross to the other side ("although why anybody would want to flee," he said, "when everything's turning out for the best"). That same evening he spoke warmly about Nagy's determined attitude towards the Russians and closer links with the West. The next day he listed in detail for her all the necessities the students had managed to collect ("purely a safety measure," he assured her, "nothing more"). An enormous supply, he declared proudly, as if these acquired successes, in some paradoxical way, manifested themselves in just those collected necessities and those piles of clothes ("you can't imagine…"), those piles of shirts, jerseys, coats, underwear and scarves, of the most varied headgear, shoes, boots and in those piles of boxes of medicine, bandages and all sorts of medical articles, not forgetting all the cases of tins, flour bags, potatoes and fresh maize.

"And beer," he added. "There's plenty of beer and cigarettes."

Towards Wednesday evening it grew colder (it really was unusually cold for the time of year), the temperature dropped further during the night and when they awoke on Thursday morning it was overcast and the ground was covered in frost. For the first time since the rising had started, as if by a strange whim of fate, the usual food delivery from Sopron did not arrive. Nor did the lorry from Görbehalom Telep village turn up, which usually came every Thursday with eggs, milk and fresh vegetables. When Dóra looked into the matter it emerged that the farmers had started hoarding. She decided therefore that they would replace supper with warm bread and milk, and, since their coal supply had also diminished considerably that they would no longer heat more than two of the dormitories, the smallest classroom and their own rooms. In the evening the temperature had dropped so much that they had to wear their outdoor clothes indoors.

Oddly enough none of the children complained.

The little boy remained silently by her side the whole time, whilst the girls were if anything livelier than usual, almost euphoric. It wasn't until they were already in bed that Agnes suddenly asked whether it was true that there was a war in Budapest and whether that was why the other girls (as well as the cook and the older teachers) had gone home in the middle of term while they had had to stay behind.

So strange, it passed through her mind, so strange that none of the girls had asked that earlier.

When Maria immediately afterwards turned out the light in the dormitory you could hear Erzsébet whispering in the darkness to Agnes about her mummy. Erzsébet, Magda thought. Little Erzsébet.

Oh, little Erzsébet, she thought again the next day in the school hall (Erzsébet was busy reading a poem to the class "one of the most beautiful poems ever written in the Hungarian language" – that was how Magda had introduced it to them), and she was amazed that the girl's voice in some indefined and wonderful way seemed to combine the darkness of the night not only with the pale sunlight which was reflected in her desktop and for a brief moment brightened up the dirty yellow plaster of the walls, but also with the acrid smell of wet chalk, with the boy's light breathing (he was sleeping with his head resting against the desktop and his mouth wide open) and with the girls' upturned faces, brown dresses, white collars, yellow hairbands, plaits and demurely folded hands – oh, little Erzsébet, she thought, she reads so monotonously, so artlessly and yet so wholly irresistibly! And it occurred to her that she would like to take Attila József's words one by one and distribute them among the girls, like handing out painted eggs at Easter, she thought happily (for despite everything that had happened she did really feel happy at that moment) – just as if they were eggs. Pigeons' eggs, she thought, for now she suddenly remembered her grandfather's voice in the pigeon loft and the egg he allowed her to hold just for a moment before putting it back into the nest, she remembered her breathless joy blended with horror (she had of course been terrified that she would crush it).

Oh, little Erzsébet, she thought (at the very moment the open window at the back of the classroom banged shut and Erzsébet with flushed cheeks closed her book and returned to her desk) – and she leaned forward over her teacher's desk.

Waited.

"One of those azure blue duvet covers," exclaimed Agnes and the gap between her front teeth became an exclamation mark. "I've always wanted one of those azure blue covers myself."

Magda then asked if they liked the poem. They did. Although, they said, they couldn't understand what Death had to do with it. Why Death wanted to make soup of the writer's poems.

Death?

Before she had time to answer Erzsébet got up and declared in a whisper that personally she loved bean soup. "A really thick, hot soup with large bits of boiled ham."

"Just the kind of soup," she added before sinking back down on to her bench, "that my mother used to make for my name day".

Magda was seized by a desire to hug her.

Oh, she thought, they really had understood.

Aloud she said: "Eva, it's your turn to read," and in the same breath she told them about the poem they were about to hear.

She mentioned when it was written, that the writer's poem was a homage to another great writer of the time, that at first it was forbidden by the censors but that nevertheless it had gradually been allowed to be printed. "He wrote it," she said, and it struck her at that moment that the girls, who were now all looking at her, exuded the very same concentration and seriousness as they usually did when they were playing hopscotch in the schoolyard, "he wrote it in a single night surrounded by his friends".

Eva began to read.

And now something completely unexpected happened. When Magda (for the umpteenth time) heard this poem being read again, when Eva lisping shyly and obviously at the same time both amused and proud, projected the picture of the little child in its bed listening to the tales of the storyteller, she was reminded suddenly of her mother – indeed, she saw all at once, with an overwhelming clarity, the figure of her mother before her. Her mother was sitting on the edge of the bed dressed in black and with a very straight back, on her lap she was holding the book of *Mary Poppins* and she was reading with an earnest, concentrated expression the chapter that Magda always loved more than all the others: the story of how Mary on her day off, together with her fiancé Bert, disappeared into a picture, into the fairground that Bert had painted somewhere on a pavement in central London. She saw again Mary and Bert climbing through the picture into the wonderful fairground, saw them riding on a merry-go-round and having tea with jam cakes (deliciously good jam cakes that melted in your mouth) and it struck her that just this story and particularly of course the actual moment of transition had always filled her with such strong and contradictory emotions, with both quivering anticipation, piety, and happiness as well as the most terrible sorrow. And it struck her at the same time that the fact that she didn't really have any nore immediate mental picture of her mother than that of her

16

there on the edge of the bed, and in some dim fashion it made her mother embody the actual focus of the tale, the invisible boundary between life and poetry- and then not only the magical moment of transition but also, in at least as great a measure, the sorrowful moment when Mary and Bert left the fairground and the picture was washed away for ever by a sudden downpour. So sad, she thought (just as the sound of the girl's feeble voice reached her again).

So terribly sad.

I love these girls, she then thought (and wondered if they would remember these poems they had heard today, if after all they would preserve the images and metaphors, the rhythms, the sounds and the skilful rhymes somewhere in the depth of their hearts) – I love them all – chubby little Erzsébet, the weasel-quick Agnes, Eva, Barbara, Zsofi and all the others.

Sándor rang late that same evening. First he asked her, as he had done ever since last Monday, to try to get in to Sopron: "I simply must meet you." After that he told her quite briefly about the latest rumours: there had been a terrible massacre at Magyaróvár with hundreds of wounded and dead, many of them children. But that was several days ago and soon all that would be over – the Russians, he knew from reliable sources, really were now on the point of leaving the country.

Magyaróvár, Magda thought. And instead she asked quickly: "Are you playing?"

Sándor sounded surprised. Of course he was playing. A lot. Indeed even more often and more regularly than normal. Liszt especially, of course, just now the Scherzo and March. He loved that piece, he said, for its boldness and finesse, because you could see the duality in Liszt's nature, the strange contradictions and the revolutionary spirit that infused all his music. Naturally he was playing – it was only now, only these last few days that he would seriously start to plan for the future. "When all this is over," he said, "you and I shall go to Vienna. To Vienna – and then on to Paris, Milan and Rome."

The conversation ended soon after that.

After putting down the receiver, Magda sat for a long time with her hand on the phone. Magyaróvár? she thought. Why Magyróvár in particular? – and decided at that moment to do something she hadn't done for two years: she looked up the number and rang her aunt in Budapest.

Her aunt answered on the first ring. She sounded pleasantly surprised when she recognized her niece's voice. "My dear," she cried, "how are you?" The last time Magda had met her aunt had been at her uncle's funeral at Györ, just before her aunt had moved with her son to Pest. She had worn a black coat then, a black hat and an unusually matted and moth-eaten fox fur, and when Magda now talked to her, she could see her just as she was then: while her aunt talked about her aches and pains and the difficulty in getting hold of nice knitting wool in the same slightly confused, vague way as about the present situation in the capital; indeed, in the same breath she mentioned the cardigan she was busy knitting and the fact that her son had left home two days ago and she didn't know where, and that there was awful shooting and that she herself was scared to death even just going to Czemege to buy bread. Magda could see in her mind's eye how, with a thoughtful expression, she let her fingertips glide over the almost bald fox's head where the eye sockets gleamed vacantly and the teeth had fallen out long ago.

"There is something odd about the radio too," her aunt said. "They're obviously not broadcasting news any longer, because when you tune in you come into the middle of the Nutcracker Suite."

All through their conversation Magda could hear the sharp ratatat of a machine-gun in the background. She urged her aunt to be careful and avoid going out. The old lady willingly promised to stay at home until everything had become calmer.

"Dear aunt, give me a ring when László's come back," Magda begged.

But what was it, she thought when she had finished the conversation, what was it I really wanted to ask her?

On the morning after her conversation with her aunt Magda awoke with an unpleasant feeling of having forgotten something, something which partly had to do with her recent dream, with its state of confusion and not least distaste, and partly with something quite different. It was just that she couldn't think what. And since at the same moment she realized that this Friday wasn't just any Friday but All Souls' Day and that she hadn't actually been in touch with her grandparents since the rising broke out, she decided that that was what she had forgotten and that she must set off for Brennbergbánya as soon as possible – after the morning's lessons, she thought (under no circumstances would she cancel her classes), by then Dóra and Maria would manage well without me.

By twelve noon she was ready to set off.

She took the delivery bicycle, not because she really hoped to get hold of anything edible in the village but because of the boy. For naturally she couldn't leave him behind at the school. He wouldn't let her out of his sight even for a moment, indeed, even if he backed away when she moved (and still remained silent) he became uneasy as soon as she did so, even for a few yards. She, though, had started to get used to his presence. It was a chilly day, grey, heavy and misty. The boy sat in the basket in front of her, wrapped in the grey floral, moth-eaten cover that Dóra used to protect the winter apples. His ears stuck out from under his cap and he had an absent look, as if he wasn't fully awake yet. It was silent and very still. The only sound was the crunching of the gravel under the bicycle tyres. There was also the barely discernible smell of smoke and of something else, something more sour, perhaps from apples about to go bad.

When they passed Görbehalom Telap a little dog came rushing out at them, a white dog with a matted coat and red-rimmed eyes. It started to bark ferociously, jumped at them from behind, and although she did her best to shoo it away it went on troubling them for at least a hundred yards, growling, yapping and howling – before finally shutting up and slinking back to the village with its tail between its legs.

Silence now descended on them again.

All the same, something had changed.

How small he is, she thought, looking at the boy sitting there in front of her, crouched under the cover and ears blood-red with the cold. And at that moment she was seized by terror, indeed, she was suddenly afraid of him, afraid of his reserve, his silence, of his not having shown by the slightest expression that he had even noticed the dog, of his merely sitting there the whole time with his back towards her, as reserved and strangely absent as ever.

Somehow, she said to herself, I must get him to speak. Somehow I have to get through to him before I'm dragged down into this terrible darkness myself.

"My grandfather," she began – and was terribly startled at the sound of her own voice.

I am speaking so loudly, she thought, as if to a deaf person.

"My grandfather," she continued in a quieter voice, "grandfather whom you will be meeting soon, was born in Brennbergbánya.

"He's lived there all his life.

"In the same white house just a stone's throw from the river."

Then she got stuck.

The boy hadn't moved a muscle. It was doubtful whether he had heard her at all. Only after a long while, at least several minutes, did she dare to start again:

"Grandmother, on the other hand, comes from somewhere else."

She waited.

He didn't move.

"She's never wanted to tell us exactly where from."

But heavens, she then thought, why am I mentioning just this? "Are you cold?" she asked instead. But as expected she didn't get any response now either.

They passed the gravel pit and then the road off that led through the forest towards Harka.

She observed him carefully: he looked so odd, she thought, with his red ears against the thin neck and his small, pale cheeks. Oh, heavens, how was she going to get him to say something? She thought she must appeal to him, ask him (for the umpteenth time) at least, if nothing else to say what his name was.

To ask for only that one thing: his name.

What am I going to do with you? she thought, as she pedalled along. What am I to do with you? – and she murmured something half-incomprehensible about her grandmother loving to listen anyway to the radio in the evenings. The path was steeper now, she was forced to stand on the pedals, and panting with exertion, she cursed herself for having taken the delivery bicycle instead of the lighter lady's bike, but anyway, she thought, what did it matter if she sounded angry, what did it matter at all what she sounded like, or what she said – "Grandfather on the other hand", she continued therefore, "detests all kinds of radio transmissions, he's done so as long as I can remember, at least since the day twelve years ago when they told him that his brother had been killed.

"Ever since that day when a colleague rang and told him that his brother had been blown up by a mine in the forest of Böhönya.

"For Grandfather", she said and now sounded almost threatening, "loved his brother more than anyone on earth".

But then, just when she finally reached the crown of the hill, she relented.

And she wanted to say something soothing. Something about the pigeons. About how her grandfather spent most of his time in his garden, in his pigeon loft nowadays. That he had two pea-cock pigeons, two fan-tails and eleven homing pigeons. But the boy didn't move and she fell silent.

She felt close to tears.

The sky had cleared and the sun cast long shadows on the road. Shortly afterwards the church came into view just in front of them. Then as she was cycling past the white building the bells began to ring. She remembered how astonished she had been the first time she had heard the peal of those bells, so much lighter than she was used to, and she thought: this is what I ought to have talked about – about the day of my seventh birth-day, and when my mother brought me here from Budapest to Brennbergbánya.

Not just for his sake, she thought. How I should have liked to tell him about that time, how different everything became, about the smell of the fermented wine and how beautiful the blue of my mother's headscarf was.

But by now they had already reached the village.

And instead she heard herself talk about the houses they were passing: there the Farkas family lived, there old Miklós, there the Csabas, "and in that large white house you can see over there, the house with the brass plate on the door, although it's empty and not much of a museum, Liszt spent part of his life there". It is, of course, she thought, and noticed that she was cycling more slowly and cautiously than before (to avoid the ducks waddling over the road, not to skid in the clay – but per-haps, too, to delay the moment when her grandparents' house would be visible on the slope down towards the stream), it is, all the same, she thought (at the moment she heard herself men-tion something about the school they had just ridden past, about the first day at that dismal village school and about the silk cloth – what on earth had that to do with the school, or with anything at all – the mauve, worn silk cloth, with long fringes, white lilies and a small monogram embroidered in each corner which her grandmother brought out for special occasions only), anyway, she thought, it's too late – and full of regret she had to ask herself why on earth she hadn't told the boy anything about her mother.

About her mother!

Well, only now (when everything really was too late) was she sure that it would have been the right thing to do; that it would have changed everything if she had had the sense to tell him about her childhood in Budapest, about her mother, about the contents of her many letters and (perhaps) even about her death.

Why had she said nothing about all that?

Perhaps all the same, she thought, so as not to make the boy uneasy – but then seemed to realize immediately afterwards that the reason was quite different: her mother's sudden death, the strange accident that occurred four years after she herself had been sent to her grandparents here in the village, had struck her from the first as quite unreal (especially as the event almost coincided with the misfortune and in a remarkably similar fashion, too) – really, she thought, it is as if my mother's visit (she was actually to have come to Brennbergbánya only a week or so after the explosion on the Margaretha Bridge) had simply been postponed temporarily and would in fact take place in the near future.

And so they had arrived.

She leaned the bicycle against the gate, lifted the boy down, took him by the hand and began to walk slowly towards the kitchen entrance at the back of the house. The garden lay silent and neglected, the ducks were nowhere to be seen and the pigeon loft doors were wide open. There was a basket of apricots standing beside the cellar steps. She picked one up, rubbed it on her coat sleeve and gave it to him.

"Dear child", she said musingly.

He accepted the apricot without looking at her. There was something so clumsy in his way of moving, something jerky that made her ashamed. and for the second time that day, just as she caught sight of her grandparents (they were standing silently just inside the doorway watching her approach) she was seized by a strong feeling of having forgotten something – but now her grandmother emerged from the semi-darkness and hurried towards them. Grandmother embraced her, kissed her, asked who the boy was she had with her and urged them before her into the house. Grandfather too seemed pleased to see her. He twiddled his moustache and absent-mindedly pinched the boy's cheek. Her grandmother at once started to prepare a meal and after an hour or so they were sitting round the table in the best room eating goulash, fried fish and cake with walnut cream. She couldn't remember when she had last eaten so much. The boy, on the other hand, didn't appear to be hungry. He played with his food, and although her grandmother (she had described vaguely how he had come to the school) showered him not just with signs of affection but with exhortations to have at least a little bit of fish, a little more cake, they hardly got anything into him. He refused, of course, to answer the old folks' questions too, not that he – sitting drawing indecipherable signs on the silken surface of the mauve cloth – seemed to be unresponsive any longer, now he seemed more confused, as if he couldn't properly understand what he was doing in this strange house. The afternoon passed otherwise in quiet gossip, a kind of restful verbal droning without beginning or end, with only the occasional pause for a slight rattle at the stove or a fairly brief radio programme (during which her grandfather took the boy with him out into the garden to show him the pigeons, which had now returned from their flight). Later she would never be able to remember what the conversation had really been about that day except for everyday topics: gossip about the neighbours, a few words about the wine harvest or the weather. Presumably her grandmother brought up the subject of Sándor and the approaching wedding too. It would have been unlike her not to. What she would come to remember was her grandmother's light voice, Grandfather's humming, the music on the radio – but on the other hand not a word about what all three were really thinking, nothing about the current situation in the country, about the uncertainty they all shared or fear of what might happen.

A slight drizzle fell towards the afternoon.

Her grandfather fetched half a sack of potatoes from the cellar (she refused to accept it at first, but he insisted). Then without a word Grandfather lifted the sack on to his shoulder and went out ahead. She wrapped the boy in the cover, kissed her grandmother quickly on the cheek, murmured something inaudible and carried the boy through the garden out to the waiting bicycle. Her grandfather helped her to settle the boy with his back against the sack of potatoes, then he held the gate open for her. Slowly she pushed the bicycle up the clayey path towards the road. When she had reached the top of the hill, just before veering off towards the village, she turned round and saw her grandfather still standing beside the gate – he was standing as she had left him, with one hand on the gate and the other raised in a farewell gesture.

Dusk now fell quickly.

When they passed the church little rows of small flames flickered in the dark: they had lit candles for the dead. It was pitch black in the forest, the bicycle's lights shone feebly and she had difficulty in making out the road in front of her, several times she nearly rode into the ditch. In Görbehalom Telep everybody seemed to be asleep. When a long time later (it must have taken her a good half hour to cover the last stretch) they approached the school building it too at first glance seemed silent, with all lights out – it wasn't until she had put the bicycle away and was crossing the dark school yard with the boy in her arms that she suddenly saw that a candle had been lit in each and every one of the building's many windows. She stood motionless.

Just like the churchyard a while ago, she thought.

At the same moment she noticed that the boy was awake and that he was staring wide-eyed at the row of points of light before him in the darkness. Then she pressed him close to her, carried him quickly over the yard, in through the door, up the dark stairs, away to her room where she undressed him and popped him into bed. Then she sat beside him and held his hand. Not until she was sure that he really was asleep did she blow out the candle in the window and go down to the kitchen.

Maria had dressed in her Sunday best. She had also spread a clean cloth on the table and decorated the chimney piece with virginia creeper. The tea-glasses were out as well as a bowl of walnuts and apricots. The trouble she had taken, together with Dóra's surly silence, filled Magda with a strange apprehension. Maria served tea. Without a word they partook of the hot, sweet drink, they cracked walnuts, tasted the apricots and refilled their tea glasses to the brim.

It was only then that she was told what had happened. "But", said Maria, "we don't, we really don't want to think the worst".

She set off early the next morning, just as they had agreed: while it was still dark outside and before any of the others were up. The boy was still asleep too. She realized that he would be in despair when he woke up and found she was gone – but what else could she do – now she simply must go in to Sopron to try to discover if the rumours were true. Since the school's lady's bicycle had a puncture she took the delivery bicycle this time too, but it wasn't until she had been cycling for quite some time that she discovered in the light from a street lamp that the floral cover was still lying in the front basket, and on top of the cover, like a dark reprimand, the boy's blue cap. She felt a slight wave of nausea and regretted not having eaten anything before setting off.

She was also freezing in the icy wind.

She passed the university campus, cycled over the railway, past the house where she had lived in her student days, straight over Petöfi tér and into the Old Town through the gateway beside Liszt Ferenc utca. In the narrow alleyways within the wall it was silent and still, it was more sheltered here too and, as always here, she experienced an overwhelming feeling of relief and liberation . She cycled slowly towards Fö tér. Not a soul was in sight, not even the coalcart, dustcart or any of the stray dogs which were usually rooting around in the backyards of the narrow streets. The market place was also deserted. A newspaper fluttered at the foot of the black iron railings round the Trinity Monument, she looked at it and thought of Sándor, imagined him standing with his back against the railings and a cigarette in the corner of his mouth – and she remembered suddenly all the occasions when she, that autumn two years ago, had waited for him just there, but not shivering with cold as on this icy November morning but squinting at the sun, at the fat grey pigeons and the fruiterers' stalls which filled the air with their sweet smell of peaches and mint. She cycled through the narrow gate by the Tower and was soon once more out on Lenin Körút, where the morning traffic was slowly beginning to build up. When she had parked her bicycle out on Szent Mihály utca she hurried away to the little alley to the house where Sándor lived. She pushed open the door, found her way up the narrow staircase, unlocked the door and went in – only to find to her surprise that Sándor wasn't at home.

Dismayed, she looked around in the room. A pale light seeped through the thin curtains, fell on the desk in front of the window and the pile of notes, paper and cigarette case, on a half-eaten slice of bread and an empty beer bottle on the piano, on the unmade bed, the pile of clothes on the floor and the stack of books against the wall. There was a smell of smoke, and through the wall a hollow cough accompanied by a peculiar scraping sound could be heard, as if something was being dragged across the floor. She hesitantly undid her coat, let it fall to the floor and went over and sat down on the edge of the bed. She remained sitting like that for some time without knowing what to do. After a while the sounds from the adjoining room ceased. And when she then caught a glimpse of her own face in the soap-smeared shaving mirror on the window ledge, when she saw the pale yellow strip of paper wedged between the glass and the brown frame, the strip on which Sándor had printed a quotation from Liszt (something Liszt had said about his life being of the sort that you had to invent in order really to understand it), and when she suddenly remembered the delight with which Sándor used to read the quotation to her, she was overpowered suddenly by a strong feeling of unreality, such a weariness that she curled up in the bed and almost immediately fell asleep. In a light slumber filled with bright happy pictures: at one moment she saw Sándor's face very close, she saw his eyes full of tenderness and desire and she felt the touch of his hand against her cheek, at the next moment they were both standing on the shore of an unknown lake – and then, at the very moment when she awoke, with crystal clarity, came the sound of his laughter.

She rose quickly from the bed, found to her horror that it was already after eleven, and that she must therefore have slept for over three hours, pulled on her coat and hurried off. It was still overcast outside, the sky was leaden grey. It had started to snow and Szeni Mihály utca was so slushy and slippery with melting snow that she left the bicycle where it was. When she came out on to Lenin Körút she couldn't believe her eyes at first. There was life and movement everywhere, doors were wide open, bundles and bags were being thrown down from open windows, people were screaming at each other, and there was a stream of people moving along the road: men with wet moustaches, expressionless faces and rattling, over-laden carts, women in black headscarves pulling similarly over-laden prams or bicycles, or children bundled up, huddled over their parents' shoulders or trudging, unsuspecting, by their side. She went a short distance down the street. When she was just about to pass Árpád, however, a large parcel fell apart and the contents fell out into the slush – a pewter container, clothes, shoes, books and a handful of letters tied with red silk ribbon.

She would never be able to remember afterwards how she actually got to know what had happened, whether she had asked around or whether one of those fleeing had noticed her confusion and of his own accord told her that a Russian force of over 700,000 men had moved towards Budapest during the night, that armoured vehicles were on their way in all directions towards Budapest, and that a large column was slowly approaching Sopron too. In any case she had realized immediately that Sándor must be out at the university and she had therefore almost running and slipping (both relieved at having just avoided being killed in the most humiliating manner by a falling parcel and sobbing with disappointment at the time she had already lost by having unintentionally fallen asleep earlier) hurried further along Lenin Körút southwards towards the university. It was difficult to make progress through the crowds on the streets and she was obliged to move aside repeatedly to make room for one of the rattling lorries on the backs of which sat old women and small children huddled together, silent, pale and expressionless. There was snow too still swirling in the air. And there was a slight smell of smoke and exhaust, and of something else, something sour and alien, which she would always associate later with the feeling of impotence that had seized her once more as she had passed the railway crossing and finally turned into Bajcsy-Zsilinszky Street and seen the red university building towering up against the leaden grey sky, when for a fraction of a second she had managed to see that the windows out on the street were boarded up, that the iron gate was shut, that there was not a soul in sight and that the only sign of life was the Hungarian flag still fluttering over the entrance.

She pushed open the gate and hurried past the flowerbed with its frostbitten dark yellow roses, stopped for a brief moment in front of the door before opening it, from indecision or perhaps from fear of what she would find inside, hesitated again, only to let it shut behind her shortly with a dull thud. For a long while she remained standing in the gloom of the hall stairway, struck by how changed it was here, how frighteningly quiet and deserted, before she finally plucked up courage again, hurried through the chilly hall and slowly, listening intently all the while and with one hand firmly holding the banister, began to mount the broad stone stairs. She found all the doors on the first floor locked. It was only on the second floor that she found one unlocked, at the furthest end of the corridor; she opened it and entered one of the large lecture halls.

The first thing she noticed when she went into the hall was not so much the cold or the dusty grey windows, not so much all the empty beer bottles on the platform or the cigarette ends on the floor below, not the coat lying thrown down over one of the front rows or even the enormous supplies at the back of the hall, all those boxes and piles of clothing that Sándor had described to her on the phone – as the fact that the silence in here seemed to be of a different nature from the one on the stairway a moment ago; that the silence suddenly seemed more restful than threatening. As if the students, Sándor among them, who had so recently convened here, those 200 students who had forged plans, shared out weapons and discussed various points in the liberation programme, had left the room only temporarily and in a short while would turn up on the threshold again, tired, drowsy, but full of vitality, and hopes for tomorrow. She took a few steps into the hall, then slid down on to the floor with her back against the platform. There she remained sitting, her arms hanging down by her sides, her legs outstretched in front of her, looking fixedly at the peeling pale blue plaster on the opposite wall; while it grew darker she tried not to think about Sándor, the photographs in his room (of the unknown woman outside her white house) and what was to happen or perhaps already had happened, when the students with the guns, molotov cocktails and the odd machine-gun got to grips with the columns of Russian armoured cars.

Sándor! She repeated his name silently to herself: Sándor, Sándor, Sándor. And she thought: he's dead, he's already been shot.

Naturally, she said to herself, naturally Sándor would be one of the first to fall.

It was quite dark when she finally got up and slowly, almost absentmindedly found her way out of the building. On the outside steps she hesitated slightly and then started back the same way she had come.

And it was then, just as she was standing, about to open the gate, that she saw it.

The body.

The body, or the young man, almost a boy (who later, although it hadn't anything to do with Sándor, would always be associated in her mind with him), the boy's body, which was hanging in the large walnut tree to the right of the university gate (oh, how thin he was, how unbearably thin, what dark, curly hair he had, what a large nose and such remarkably slender wrists!) and moving gently in the breeze like a huge black clapper in an invisible bell. She saw the rope which had bitten into his neck, saw one eye almost gouged out of its socket and staring blindly up at the sky, saw the other, of which only a few fleshy tatters remained, the blueish black swollen tongue so full of slash marks and the leaflet (where someone had written the initials of the secret police) tied to the navy-blue jacket sleeve. And she noticed, as the distant and surprising rattle of a train reached her, that one of the boy's hands, the right one which up to now had been hidden from her view, had caught in one of the branches of the tree – as if he hadn't quite decided whether to find the time to pick a handful of walnuts, crack them with his teeth and eat them or to continue his walk at once towards the city centre.

Later she would never know she spent the rest of that day.

Or even the night.

The only thing she would remember with certainty was that she returned to the school on Sunday morning, that the ground was covered in snow and that the first thing she caught sight of when she led the delivery bicycle across the school yard was the boy, who was sitting in the window of her room with his face pressed against the pane.

That he was sitting there.

And that his face lit up when he caught sight of her.

An hour or so later they were all assembled in the dining room.

"Today," Maria said, letting her eye sweep over the thirteen girls eating their porridge, "today really is the day".

The sun shone through the window. Dóra, who had just returned from Mass with the girls (it was a miracle, Magda thought, that she succeeded in getting back and forth to church without mishap and that Mass was celebrated at all that Sunday when Sopron had finally fallen) raised her head from her clasped hands, made the sign of the cross and looked at Magda with strangely glistening eyes: "Yes," she said. "Maria's right. Today we're finally going on the excursion up into the mountains that you've dreamt of for so long."

The girls' delight knew no bounds. They shouted for joy, clapped their hands and began at once to discuss what they would take with them, whether they would perhaps find some secret grotto and what sorts of mushrooms they would be able to pick.

"Slippery jacks and ceps and giant puffballs," Agnes shouted.

"And lovely small russulas," Erzsébet said dreamily.

Maria gave a faint smile.

"It's been snowing," she said. "The ground's quite white."

The girls looked at her in amazement.

"Not in the forest," Agnes maintained resolutely.

"Maize," Erzsébet continued with the same dreamy expression as before. "We can take some maize with us and roast it over an open fire."

After that the girls cast themselves over their porridge, said their thank yous and disappeared up into the dormitory.

It grew silent round the table and Maria got up and began to clear things away. Dóra sat with both hands tightly clenched around her body and her grey birdlike head sunk down between her narrow shoulders. "We'll leave in an hour," she said. Then she straightened herself up: "Magda," she went on. "You haven't heard everything."

She then explained that it wasn't just the terrible things being played out in Budapest which had finally made her reach her decision. Not only the massacre in Magyaróvár. Not even, first and foremost, that Sopron too had now fallen and people were fleeing in their thousands.

No, yesterday evening, she said in a strangely hesitant tone, yesterday another rumour had reached them.

And that rumour – well, it no longer left them any choice.

Here she paused for a moment as if to gather strength.

In Várpalota, she then said, the Russians had attacked a school. Two hundred children, all under twelve, had been killed, and the rest, perhaps a hundred, had been taken off in lorries, in all probability to Russia.

Did she understand what that meant? Dóra wondered.

If they now delayed the same fate would in all probability befall their girls too. She had therefore been trying all night to

33

get hold of the girls' parents – but, as before, in vain. Now, she said, they must save the children themselves. The one thing, indeed the only thing they could hope for, was that the children would find their parents again on the other side of the border.

Here she fell silent and looked up.

And at the very moment that Magda met her glistening eyes it occurred to her that Dóra was not only terrified, not only convinced of what she had to do and firmly determined to do what was expected of her, she was also deeply sorrowful.

Or rather – heartbroken!

Well, she soon understood it: to flee, to leave your country and the district where you had spent every day of your fifty-five years so far, that for Dóra didn't signify choosing liberty, it meant choosing not life but – death. Magda realized too, however, that nothing would make her change her mind. And when shortly afterwards they left the school it was in fact Dóra who checked that the door was locked, the outhouses shut up and that the gate was properly closed behind them. And she it was who had seen to it that the girls had their hair neatly plaited and, as they trotted along hand in hand, that their bright yellow bows were clean and freshly ironed and that their small rucksacks were filled not just with food (a piece of bread, two winter apples, a handful of walnuts and two thin slices of smoked sausage, all of which, it later emerged, Dóra had succeeded in obtaining the previous evening in Görbehalom Telep in exchange for an amethyst brooch she had inherited from her mother) but also with equipment which might be needed on the excursion up in the mountains: a small spade, a magnifying glass, a notebook and a pen.

Dóra was really beside herself with fear, that was obvious.

But she was also strangely exhilarated. She repeatedly assured the girls of how splendid a time they would have on their outing, how many mushrooms they would pick, how many beautiful things they would see – and finally she began to sing.

So loudly, so out of tune and with such an obvious aim that it was a miracle that the girls not only joined in the hymn but were also infected by its cheerful melody, began to observe everything about them with the same unfeigned delight, the clear blue sky, the sun which was already warming slightly, the glittering tree tops, the croaking of the crows in the fir trees by the roadside and, not least, the funny imprint of their small boots in the white snow – as surprising as when Agnes and Erzsébet, when they all together, still in neat two-by-two columns, turned off to the right at the first crossroads about half a mile from the school and began to walk through Görbehalom Telep, shouted simultaneously that (a complete impossibility) they could already see the mountains silhouetted like a blue streak on the horizon.

2

The old cadet college in Traiskirchen, where they arrived long after dark one and a half days later, emerged in the pale morning light; as well as the large main building (a huge yellowish-grey stone complex where they had been housed in a gymnasium on the third floor), it consisted of a spacious gravelled barrack square, a long, fairly low yellow house, a one-storeyed house in the same dreary colour as the main building and beyond the barrack square a lawn and something that looked like the remains of an intersecting avenue. Soon enough they also noticed that around the whole area rose a high, spiked iron fence, a fence which turned into a yellow brick wall six feet high just at the end of the avenue.

Inside the camp utter chaos reigned.

It was impossible to say how many refugees had been led here, perhaps several thousand. The crowding was terrible, everybody seemed to be confused and terrified, nobody seemed to know anything, not even the weary helpers who now and then hurried past and in answer to every question shook their heads evasively and with a vague gesture pointed towards the crowd of well-padded figures.

"We're sorry!" they said. "We're sorry – but what can we do?

"Go and see the medical staff, perhaps they can answer your questions.

"Try in the yellow building over there. Or rather, stay where you are and wait for further instructions."

It was so crowded in the gymnasium that you could hardly manage to get through. The floor was covered with straw ("What should we have done if the farmers hadn't been so obliging?") and even though there was a high ceiling it was difficult to breathe: not only was the air permeated with the smoke from the old stove and the nauseating smell of unwashed bodies and damp wool, but it was also thick with all the dust that had been shaken out of the straw and made eyes and throat smart. The coal stove, moreover, produced no real heat, the walls were of stone, the window frames didn't fit, there was an icy draught and their teeth chattered as they sat cowering under their blankets, waiting.

They were also very hungry.

The girls are so silent, she thought. Why don't they say something? Why don't they ask anything about what's going to happen now?

Their first meal wasn't served until about twelve o'clock.

"We're sorry," the women with white armbands now repeated as they served soup, bread and mugs of weak sweetened tea out on the barrack square (there was also a keen wind and the chill gave every spoonful of soup and every bite of bread an insipid tinny taste). "But," they continued, while informing them about the routine at the camp and pointing out where the newly installed latrines were situated, "everything will get better soon". And they assured them that everywhere in Europe the Red Cross was working flat out, that food was on its way, as well as medicine and clothes – while in the same breath pointing out with a slight shrug of the shoulders that Traiskirchen wasn't really a place where anybody should stay, that the camp was nothing more than a transit camp, only the first step to a better life.

The way they said it confused her:

"A better life!"

38

"A life of freedom!"

But wasn't there something strangely ambivalent in their voice? A note not only of sympathy but also of something else – something which surely most of all resembled contempt?

In the afternoon they were summoned to be registered in an office provisionally installed on the ground floor of the main building. Three men sat behind a table in the room, one in uniform, one in a long grey overcoat (he was the one who made notes) and one who acted as interpreter.

There was a queue in front of the table.

After a wait of about half an hour it was their turn. Dóra produced their three passports and a list of the girls which she had obviously already drawn up on the evening before they had left, a list of the girls' names, the names of their parents, their birthplace, their home addresses and their father's profession. The man in uniform then called the girls, one by one, the man in grey transferred their names into his book, requested them to confirm the details and asked Dóra very discreetly:

"The children's parents?"

When Dóra shook her head he shrugged regretfully and noted something in his book beside the girls' names.

Magda herself waited until last with the boy in her arms.

What shall I say? she thought. What shall I say when they ask what he's called?

Then it was her turn. She confirmed that the details in her passport were correct, explained that she had lived in Budapest until she was nine and then with her grandparents in the village of Brennbergbánya, but that for the last three years the school had been her fixed address.

A note was made of everything she said.

"Is it true the child's not your son?" wondered the man in the grey coat.

She nodded, surprised. Had Dóra included that information on her list?

"That's so," she clarified, "The boy isn't my child."

"That's right," she repeated, pressing the boy more closely towards her: "He's not my son."

At that moment she was seized by a kind of rage, indeed of disgust, at the three men's friendly and sympathetic smiles, and to her surprise she suddenly heard herself say – in a considerably louder voice than before: "József Attila."

Yes indeed, just like that!

"He was born on 27 October 1952 (it was so wonderfully easy to lie! and naturally – the 27th, after all, that was when everything started!). "He came to our school quite recently – and his name is in fact: József Attila."

And yet the most ludicrous thing of all she was to think later when it was all over, perhaps the most ludicrous thing wasn't their ignorance. Not the fact that they – naturally – understood nothing, that neither the poor official in uniform, the man in grey nor even the interpreter seemed to understand what she had really said, but had merely nodded benignly, all three, and noted the name in their papers. But not even the fact that, when half amused, half tearfully she muttered something about József Attila being not any old name but the name of a famous poet, they merely nodded yet again and explained that they would do everything in their power to arrange matters for the best. No, she was to think later, the most ludicrous thing was that on top of everything else they'd misunderstood the name.

They'd written the surname where the forename should be.

And thus given the boy a different first name from the one she had intended.

"Tomorrow morning," that was what they had shouted to her just as she was on the point of leaving the office, "some time early tomorrow the children are to have a medical examination. Please take little József to the yellow building at about eight o'clock!"

40

The second day was like the first. Except for a few short breaks for food, queuing for the few washrooms or for the sick room, they spent most of their time in a corner of the dormitory huddled up in the blankets, dozing – but at the same time filled with a vague feeling that there was something they ought to be doing.

Something – but what?

The third day passed, just as the fourth and the fifth – indeed they found it increasingly difficult to distinguish the days, soon they all ran into each other, everything became a single, grey, tedious waiting. The waiting was like a strange, gnawing, never-sated feeling of simultaneous hunger and lack of appetite.

Then gradually it started to snow too.

Sándor, she thought, looking at the light, sparse snowflakes twirling slowly towards the ground and immediately dissolving in the dark grass and vanishing.

Sándor?

Unless now…?

Unless the girls…?

No…

And she wondered why it was that the girls were always silent.

That they seemed to withdraw more and more.

And that they still hadn't uttered a single enquiring word about how this strange excursion was going to end.

Is it a fact, she wondered, and the thought filled her with real horror, is it perhaps really a fact that the girls still consider this as simply – an excursion? Do the girls in actual fact think that we're all soon, very soon, going back home? Hasn't Dóra told them anything?

I must ask her.

By tomorrow we must decide what we are going to do.

From her bunk over in the furthest corner of the gymnasium right next to the window she could catch a glimpse of the iron railings and the deserted village street outside, she could see that hazel thicket which grew just where the fence became a wall, she could see the sparse tree trunks in the avenue and, most important, she could see into the park which opened out beyond.

Oh, that park!

That park! she thought. It is as if it wanted to remind me of something – but what?

It was a large park, from the fourth-storey window it could seem almost endless – indeed, it was very easy to imagine (but impossible to know because of the yellow brick wall) that it merged into the blue mountain range in the distance – or rather: into the wooded slopes at the foot of the mountain.

The park is enticing, she often thought while observing the pale daylight filter like thin smoke through the dark treetops, letting her eye glide over the shiny-black rough trunks and the diffuse pattern of the shadows in the foliage.

Enticing – although in a melancholy way.

But just because it was so melancholy, just because of that, she liked to try imagining what it would be like to walk through it (which in reality, for some inexplicable reason, she still couldn't force herself to do) she liked in her mind's eye to let herself be engulfed by the silence of the park, by the peace, the damp haze and the smell of earth and mouldering leaves. Indeed, in her imagination she liked to let herself disappear into the darkness of the park – just as it pleased her to imagine the girls there.

The girls and the boy!

"Come on!" That's what one of them, Agnes or Erzsébet would say, she thought.

"Come on, József!"

And at once in her mind's eye she saw how the boy bravely and unhesitatingly accompanied the girls in among the trees – so far in that nobody could find them any longer. She saw how

42

altogether, two by two and hand in hand, they found their way along an unknown path in there, how, with loud laughter and delight at the bold antics of the squirrels, the sighing wind in the trees and the giant-like crows' nests way above their heads (which she thought reminded her most movingly of the clumsy darns in her grandmother's black Sunday shawl), they filled their pockets with half-decayed rose hips and finally tired out but satisfied sat down to rest in a clearing among the trees.

Well, she thought, the park would not only entice them to forget – forget everything they never talk about but which surely occupies all their thoughts.

It would also entice them to play.

The street outside the iron gate lay deserted and empty. There was not a soul to be seen, not even in the small gardens around the houses on the opposite side of the street.

It struck her that she had never caught a glimpse of a living being in those houses – it is, she sometimes thought, as if life out there had completely ceased to exist.

Now she observed the boy sitting hunched up in the low window-recess, looking out.

József, she thought. József – and at that moment she noticed that his left ear not only stood out more than the right, as she had discovered a long time ago, but that it was also shinier and without any lobe at all.

She got up and went over to him.

He didn't move, didn't show in the slightest that he was aware of her standing there but continued with an absent-minded expression to watch the snowflakes' slow dance towards the ground.

Then she raised her hand and stroked his hair.

Let her hand glide in a caress over the thin nape of the neck and rest on his shoulder – but not even then did he turn around and meet her gaze.

Dusk fell.

The night that followed was pitch black and without stars.

Then early next morning the sun broke through.

Now is the time, it flashed through her consciousness, now is the time I ought to find the refugees who are new to the camp, now I ought to ask these newly arrived refugees if they know anything about Sándor.

About Sándor – or about the girls' parents!

And yet she didn't do so. No, she couldn't make herself do any of the things she had decided to do.

The street out there still lay deserted – and she thought that the trouble was not only that she had lost her grip on time (that in fact she no longer knew for certain how much time had elapsed since they had come to the camp, if it was only a single week or if it was two, perhaps even three): the trouble was that she could no longer see the point of the whole thing.

Everything seemed so senseless.

Admittedly since they had crossed the border Maria had been full of confidence in the future.

Dóra, however, grew more silent day by day.

Just like the girls.

She felt such disgust at the whole thing, disgust and a completely paralysing weariness.

Later that day or perhaps the next she suddenly saw the girls through the window playing over by the hazel thicket.

Was playing what they were really doing?

If they now didn't …?

If they didn't…?

It is, she thought, more as if they were performing some kind of secret rite.

Indeed the girls seemed to her at that moment suddenly more alien than at any time earlier!

So serious and so impossible to fathom!

And she thought that the game they were playing, if it now was a question of a game at all, wasn't in any case one that she recognized: she couldn't even guess its import, could neither interpret the girls' gestures or expression, nor for that matter the movements which seemed to be executed with such a languid and positively uncanny precision. A stone – or a ball (wherever could they have got that from?) – seemed to play a certain role, similarly a broken branch, small jumps in different directions, perhaps a rhyme of some sort too: she couldn't hear anything but she could see very clearly how each one of them in some sort of incomprehensible order formed their lips into something that must have been words.

If they didn't now? she again thought.

If they didn't...?

And if only it weren't so cold! If only the air in the dormitory weren't so stuffy, Maria so unnaturally and cheerfully dismissive and Dóra so silent! The following night she had a dream, a vague and strangely indistinct dream. When she awoke it had started to snow again.

Harder now.

The ground was already gleaming white between the trees.

Shortly after that she heard Erzsébet's voice: "Come on! Come on, József!"

She turned round quickly – and to her surprise saw how the boy unravelled himself from his blanket, how he took Erzrébet's outstretched hand and how, through the crowd of young children, breast-feeding mothers, men chewing their pipes and dozing old people, he allowed himself to be led out of the room's semi-darkness.

I ought to...it occurred to her.

Perhaps I ought to...

But she hadn't had time to think the thought through before she saw the girls appear over by the avenue with the boy between them.

The children trudged slowly through the snow. They stopped beside the hazel thicket and formed a semi-circle which seemed to mark the beginning of the game.

She noticed how, hesitantly, the boy kept slightly behind Erzsébet.

How he remained behind her throughout all the moves of the game and how, when they returned to the camp he followed her constantly like a shadow.

Just as serious as she was.

As serious and with the same unfathomable expression studying the tracks of his boots in the snow.

Then she saw all this repeated the following day and again the next day.

It was only on the third day that she observed that the boy dared to let go of Erzsébet's hand.

On the fourth day he took a step towards Agnes and Zsofi.

On the fifth day he gave a little jump to the side and clapped his hands. Now she saw how he too caught the stone (or perhaps it might have been a ball) when it was thrown to him, and how he in his turn passed it on.

And she saw, there was really no doubt about it, she saw how not only on one but on several occasions – in the strange, perplexing sequence which seemed to apply – he opened his mouth and uttered a few words.

The boy had started to talk!

Yes, he really had started to talk!

The fact that the boy had spoken, she now often thought, is remarkable enough.

And yet – there was more to it, of course.

He seemed to have accepted his name too.

He acted as though he really was called József.

As if his name was Jozsef!

Unless, she thought (and the thought filled her with dismay) unless that really is what he is called.

Unless his name really is József, which in fact is quite possible.

"József," Agnes asked sleepily one evening, "József, do you remember?"

"Ye-e-s," the boy's voice was heard in the darkness.

"József," whispered Erasébet a while later, "József, are you asleep?"

The days passed. It continued to snow. It also grew appreciably colder.

They now felt the cold generally more than ever.

But the food had improved. A real goulash with meat, onions and peppers once replaced the pea soup. Once apples were shared out. On another occasion every one of them received a handful of blue plums.

Early one morning nevertheless she thought she caught sight of someone outside in the village street – but she wasn't certain. Perhaps it was only a mirage.

Dóra hardly uttered a word by now.

It is, she sometimes thought, as if Dóra with her silence wants to achieve something.

If only I could understand what.

But then suddenly it was all too late!

Indeed suddenly everything was really too late – sometime in the middle of December Erzsébet disappeared.

Early one morning, they were all gathered on the barrack square, except for Dóra (who was still lying on her mattress in the semi-darkness of the dormitory, as motionless and withdrawn as ever) and they saw Erzsébet with an address label around her neck (a hand-written label with name and destination: Memphis, Tennessee) being led to the waiting Red Cross bus by a woman in a green loden jacket, a Tyrolean hat and white armband.

Erzsébet hadn't asked anything.

And now she didn't cry, she didn't even seem afraid. The only thing her face expressed was bewilderment. Bewilderment and a kind of wide-eyed surprise.

In her right hand she held the orange someone had pushed into it, her coat belt as usual was drawn tightly over her round tummy.

The woman in the loden jacket helped Erzsébet on to the bus.

And without turning to wave, so Erzsébet vanished from their lives for ever.

Only a day or two later it was Agnes' turn (she had been adopted by a family somewhere outside London).

Agnes too was given an orange.

Agnes too was led by the woman in a loden jacket over the barrack square to the waiting Red Cross bus.

Agnes too vanished without waving.

A few more days passed: then Eva disappeared (to Amsterdam or perhaps Denmark), then Barbara, Zsofi and the rest of the girls.

Maria too – on Christmas Eve itself.

It really was on Christmas Eve, the very evening of 24 December, that Maria left the camp – overjoyed and repeatedly counting her blessings (she had got a job as a hotel cleaner in Graz) -she kissed Magda goodbye and asked her to write. And, as if by a trick of fate, it was the same evening that Dóra, feverish, dehydrated and semi-conscious, was taken by ambulance from the camp to a hospital somewhere north of Vienna. So, seven weeks almost to the day since their arrival at the camp, only she and the boy were left.

Only me, she thought, only me and József.

A week or so later, at the beginning of January, she took József with her for the first time for a walk outside the camp. As well as looking around, she thought, they would also (since the previous evening she had managed to exchange her 200 forint for almost 400 Austrian schilling) try to find the village café.

They walked along the village street to the right of the gates, followed the iron railings and then the yellow brick wall westwards towards the forest and the mountains. A dog barked somewhere in the far distance, otherwise the houses and small gardens looked deserted as usual. It was a still day, chilly and slightly damp. In the pale sunlight the snow shone with an intense, almost unnatural brilliance.

She held József's hand. They walked in silence.

After a while, before they had even glimpsed the end of the wall, they turned and went back the same way they had come. They passed the gates again, nodded to the guard who was half-asleep, and carried on down the street, in towards the village centre. At the first crossing they met a little girl in a blue beret and a school satchel on her back, after two further crossroads they had arrived at the railway crossing. To the left, a short distance away, lay the yellow station building.

The clock above the entrance showed twenty minutes past one.

They stood for a while waiting, hesitant. But nothing happened, everything was quiet and dead, there were no travellers visible, neither in the waiting room doorway nor out on the platform. Then they turned once more, went back along the same street, passed the first crossing, the second – and then suddenly they discovered the café in the low white house with brown window frames only a hundred yards or so from the camp itself.

A bell tinkled when they opened the door. Inside it smelt of smoke, smoke and sour wine. They sat down at a table nearest the window. Apart from an old man in a brown checked cap and black scarf they were the only customers.

In front of the counter lay a dog, dozing with its head resting on its paws, a huge dog with a white coat, dirty and matted like an old polar bear's.

They waited. József sat still with his hands clasped on his lap.

The woman who suddenly appeared in the doorway behind the counter was large and fat, and her hair was fastened in a huge bun She was dressed in a shiny, navy dress, had a white apron tied around her stomach and when she approached their table she smiled with her whole face.

Magda ordered.

The woman soon returned. She put the cup of coffee in front of Magda, the glass of orange juice and the square piece of apple tart in front of József. But then she didn't leave them but remained, introduced herself as Frau Edith and explained that it was her husband who owned the café. She asked where they came from, how long they had lived in the camp and why they had never been here before. When she noticed that József had finished his juice and picked at the last pie crumbs she urged him to go over and pat the dog.

"He's a good dog," she said, kindly, "Don't be frightened."

After a certain hesitation József did as she said, he slid from the chair and took a few steps towards the dog. Both women followed him with their eyes. When he knelt down beside the dog and cautiously stretched out his hand towards it Frau Edith sank down with a contented sigh on the chair beside Magda.

"Ach ja", she sighed, "Ach ja…"

Then she explained that her husband was from Romania, while she herself was born and bred here in Traiskirchen, she told Magda that she had two children, two boys who were grown up now and who both worked on the railway, that she loved the café, that she baked most of the bread herself but that she wished they could have more customers.

And she asked Magda in her turn to describe what it had been like when she had got across the border.

"For you seem able to speak German. Some, at least."

Magda nodded. But so strange, she thought, that that language sounds so different out of the mouth of the fat woman here in the café, than at the camp. So much lighter and more transparent, somehow. "The escape?" she said evasively. "No, I can't remember very much about the actual escape" – and it occurred to her at that moment that what she said was actually true. It was really, she thought in amazement, as if Maria, Dóra, I, the boy and all thirteen girls from the village of Görbehalom Telep had strayed straight into total darkness.

Frau Edith laughed slightly.

She raised a plump finger and pointed: József had thrown both arms around the dog's neck and buried his chin in its dirty white coat. The dog lay still but it thumped the floor rhythmically with its thick long tail.

Frau Edith laughed even more.

"Ah," she said, "I could see at once! Your son loves dogs!"

Magda looked at her in surprise. Then she quickly ran her hand over her hair.

"Yes," she said. "He loves dogs. He always has. József loved dogs long before he was walking."

"Dogs are a blessing," sighed Frau Edith, "and sons".

Magda nodded.

"Yes," she said. "It's a blessing to have a son."

From then on she and József visited the café every day. They always went the same way, followed the wall first to the right, then turned and walked along the street all the way to the railway crossing, where they stood for a while and looked around before going back the same way to the white house with the

brown windows. They didn't go there so much to order anything – never had more than a glass of fruit juice, sometimes a
cup of coffee (the money she had amounted to a mere pittance
despite everything) – as to talk.

Or rather: to listen.

It was mostly Frau Edith who held forth. While József drank
his juice, fiddled with the tablecloth, patted the dog or busied
himself with the toys, rather the worse for wear, she had found
among the things her sons had left (a few tin soldiers, a paper
doll without clothes and a small green engine) Frau Edith talked
about her childhood here in the village. With her eyes full of
tears she told them about her father who had been a blacksmith
and who used to give her a hiding during the week, admittedly,
but who almost every Sunday gave her a little bag of sweets, who
had lost his hearing in one ear in the First World War and who
had died in the Second, "although by that time I'd already been
married for some time, of course, and had the two little ones as
my comfort". She described proudly the vegetables she and her
mother had grown, "the pumpkins – you should have seen
them!", she mentioned the school mistress at that time "the
nicest person I have ever met!" and sighed at the memory of her
first communion.

Magda herself just didn't think she had anything to talk
about. And she was for the most part content to listen, asked a
question now and then and smile gratefully when Frau Edith on
occasion praised her German pronunciation.

"Mind you, you don't speak without mistakes," she said.
"But everything you say sounds so – elegant."

It was really only when Frau Edith brought up the subject of
her sons that any real conversation arose between them. When
they talked about Jozsef's childhood Magda suddenly had a
great deal to say.

"Anyway," laughed Frau Edith, "where the boy's concerned
there's nothing wrong with your memory".

"Added to which," she said, "it's funny to see how much he resembles you. The little lad's the image of you!"

Late one afternoon when Magda and József were on their way back to the camp József asked what she and Frau Edith had actually been talking about there in the café – and for the first time it struck her that he hadn't really understood a word of their conversation.

The sun had already sunk low and the poplars were casting long blue shadows over the snow.

She laughed slightly.

"Frau Edith was telling me about her cousin," she said. "Frau Edith's cousin is married to the station master and their cat is the best rat-catcher in the whole village."

Then she hesitated.

"But we were talking about you too," she then went on. "I said that you've always been interested in trains, especially steam engines, and then I mentioned something about your once – although you were too small to remember it – having taken the train all the way to Budapest."

They walked ten yards or so in silence. József wiped his nose repeatedly on his mitten. When they passed the lamp post just opposite the café he stretched out his hand absentmindedly and touched it. It wasn't until they were almost back at the camp gates that he raised his head and looked at her: "Oh yes," he said firmly, "I remember that.

"Yes, going by train to Budapest – I remember that distinctly.

"We were sitting opposite each other," he said.

"You and I," he said, and now he sounded almost stern. "We had dripping and paprika sandwiches. And then when we'd eaten I fell asleep with my head it your lap.

"Although, of course," he added just as they went in through the gates, "you were also little then, about like Erzsébet."

From then on, when their walks took them to the railway crossing they always looked around with special attention, they lingered longer than usual at the raised booms, waiting for a train that must surely come some time, and after a while they began to expand their walks to include the station itself.

They approached the yellow, seemingly deserted building with a certain suspense.

Once there, they would first look into the waiting room, hoping to catch a glimpse of a traveller or at least the stationmaster, after which they would sit down on one of the benches outside on the platform. and out there, as they watched the rails glistening in the sun and listened to the ticking of the clock over the entrance they talked increasingly often about what it would be like the day they finally left Traiskirchen. József seemed most interested in the actual journey: he wondered a lot about what they would eat, and could sink into a reverie, wondering what colour the seats would be in the compartment.

The seats, the engine and the carriages.

But he also had views of a different kind.

We shall live in a brown house," he used to maintain, "and we shall have the same striped carpet in the kitchen as we've always had".

Gradually they began to expand their walks to cover the part of the village on the other side of the railway. While it grew warmer day by day, while the snow melted and the grass slowly turned green, they explored one street after another, they discovered the grocer's, the shoemaker's and the bicycle factory, they visited the church and they saw the children playing outside the school. They met the girl in the blue beret twice. When on the second occasion they nodded in recognition the girl smiled in return and even looked as though she was thinking of saying something before she turned and ran off.

The streets were completely deserted. They stood silently by the lowered boom at the railway crossing and waited. József clasped her hand firmly. She looked at him, he was tense and very pale: she wondered about this completely overriding interest of his, his passionate interest in anything connected with railways, not just the stationmaster (whom they had seen on several occasions by this time and even greeted, the fat, florid middle-aged man who pulled his stationmaster's cap down on his head with such self-satisfied gravity every time he left the ticket office to go out on to the platform and wave off a train, and who seemed to consider the little station as his private domain), no, not just connected with the station master but with the different trains, locomotives, signals and – in fact – the timetables that he couldn't even read himself.

Well, she thought, József's right. We must get away from here. We really must leave.

And when soon afterwards, after the train had passed, they left the railway area she suddenly found everything around them, the whole view which opened out, before them, both familiar and weirdly alien: she even suddenly had a vague feeling that it wasn't just her gaze that had changed, not only the expectations which affected her vision but also the objects themselves that surrounded her: the paving stones and the poplars, the houses with their small gardens, the lamp posts, dustbins, post boxes and the clouds.

The spring scilla were now in bloom, hallucinatory blue against the yellow brick wall. Frau Edith complained about toothache. Her cousin's cat had disappeared. József fed the dirty white dog with biscuit crumbs.

"It'll be Easter soon," Frau Edith murmured, and looked out of the windows with a distracted air. "The boys will be coming home on a visit."

The same afternoon, soon after Magda together with József

had returned to the camp, she was summoned to Herr Bauer, the camp director..

Herr Bauer looked at her kindly and explained that every-thing was now arranged for the best. "Little József", he said, "has been adopted by a family in Sweden".

Then he smiled and said that he was sure she understood, in fact he was convinced that she wouldn't oppose this decision. This decision, he said, had been reached with only one thought in mind: what was best for the boy. Of course she knew, he said, that she had no legal right at all to keep him and, he said, she must consider: what could she offer him?

She?

As a refugee?

"What could you," said Herr Bauer, "what kind of future life could you as a refugee and a single woman offer him?

"In Sweden on the other hand," he added – and now he leaned forward over the desk and looked her straight in the eye – "in Sweden the boy will be well off! A quiet and secure life! Just the kind of existence every child would wish for."

Everything happened surprisingly quickly after that. She was given sleeping pills by the camp doctor, strong pills: as in a haze she watched them come for József, saw how with an orange in one hand and a red and blue wooden horse in the other he was led by the Red Cross lady in a green loden jacket across the barrack square and out through the gate. She would never be able to remember later what she had said to him, whether she had explained anything at all to him or could even bring herself to kiss him goodbye, she had only a vague recol-lection that they had held out to him the promise of a long and exciting train journey and that he had therefore accepted everything without protest – what had transpired later, when he realized that he would be travelling alone on his journey, alone with the strange woman, or when he had gradually realized what the real purpose the journey was she daren't even contemplate.

She slept a lot. The days were warm. The light intense, piercing.

She no longer went to the café.

A few tables and chairs had been put out on the barrack square. She sat there for short periods.

But only very seldom – she spent most of the time lying on her mattress in the semi-darkness of the dormitory.

Some time towards the end of April Herr Bauer looked her up. With effusive kindness he told her that he had succeeded – at last and after much effort – in arranging employment for her.

As a music teacher – she had said that she played the piano?

At a girls' school in Vienna.

It was admittedly only temporary, the school would be closed for the term in barely two months' time, of course, but it was always something. And the rest would surely be arranged when the time came.

"You must try to forget," he said as he got up and stretched out his hand in farewell. "You must forget the past and look only to the future."

His handshake was firm, his hand cool and slightly moist.

Two hours later she departed. She was empty-handed. She had her train ticket, a small sum of money and a few addresses on a piece of paper in her coat pocket. She walked quickly, as if afraid she wouldn't get there in time, she passed the café, thought for a moment that she had heard someone call her but hurried on without turning round.

Down by the station she managed to sneak into the waiting room unseen. She sat down in a far corner, with her back to the ticket office to avoid being seen. It was warm and stuffy, a slight smell of disinfectant arose from the shiny scrubbed floor.

It was very quiet.

The minutes dragged past.

As soon as she heard the train approaching she hurried out on to the platform and boarded the only carriage with its door standing open. She was breathing heavily. When the train rolled out of the station she leaned back in her seat and closed her eyes. The sun was shining on her face, it was warm and very light.

After a short while she fell asleep.

The light! Oh, she can't remember ever having seen such lighting before: so intense and yet so veiled, so piercing and at the same time so gentle.

It is, it occurs to her, now that she is standing outside the Südbahnhof main entrance, dazzled and confused and with her body feeling strangely lightweight, it is really almost as if the boundary between herself and the town has been expunged at the very moment that she stepped out of the station. Or, she thinks, as if everything out here, the grey station building, the newspaper stall in the corner, the trams and four-storeyed houses on the other side of the street, were hovering weightlessly some distance above the ground.

She walks towards the tram stop. Asks the way and finally finds the right tram: the one that will take her in the right direction towards the address in the sixth district, Schadekgasse 16, to which the camp doctor has directed her. When soon afterwards she rides through the city, when she observes as in a trance the enormous palaces and the green parks, the churches, cars and the crowds in the street which is obviously Mariahilfer Strasse, all these impressions assail her with renewed vigour – suddenly everything she sees around her, as (strangely enough) all the promptings and the street names which the conductor calls out through his loudspeaker, make her heart beat with something akin to anticipation.

Anticipation or at least relief.

Finally! she thinks.

And indeed "finally" is the word that occurs to her when an hour or so later she enters the rented room on the second floor of Schadekgasse, and she soon finds that everything in this room – the faded wallpaper, the washbasin behind its cardboard screen, the iron stove, the large shiny wardrobe, the gauze-thin nylon lace curtains, the picture of Jesus, the narrow couch and above the bedhead the mirror on whose pale blue glass a very small cloud slowly glides out towards the black frame – corresponds in detail to the expectations she had after all.

And indeed she repeats the word later, the next morning when she enters the school gates in Glasergasse in very good time. Repeats it silently to herself, like an invocation. Or perhaps rather: confirmation. As if at that moment she really had started to forget and as if she had even begun to find something positive in the remarkable fact that just this initiation of some Viennese girls into the world of musical notation and scales, playing for them, singing with them and always teaching them new melodies, would be the introduction to her new life.

My new life!

Well, that is really what she's thinking when in the afternoon of the same day she leaves school and steps out into the sunshine in Glasergasse again.

Everything does seem to be working out!

It surprises her too that all those she has come into contact with so far have been so effusively kind. So kind and so helpful. Not just her young pupils (who have mostly been quiet and timid but nevertheless somehow kindly disposed) but also the Principal as, with her wimple drawn down over her forehead, she showed her around the school, from the mouldy-smelling store of stuffed animals and worn flower wallcharts in the basement to the art room in the attic, and similarly those teachers she has come across in the staff room or in one of the corridors, and the old caretaker who had shown her where she should sit in the schoolyard so as to be able to enjoy the shade while at the same time keeping an eye on the girls' games. They were in fact just as friendly and obliging, she thought, as the landlord yesterday evening or the greengrocer in Otto Baumer-Gasse when she picked up her bags of apples, walnuts and dried tomatoes.

So almost excessively friendly! she repeats to herself, surprised that not one of all these people has bothered about how badly she speaks (and not elegant in the least), that no-one has corrected her or even seemed to have noticed that she so often stumbles, commits the gravest grammatical errors or sometimes gets stuck altogether.

She feels genuinely grateful, is there not even something promising in all this – even in the way they address her, also? The unconstrained tone, the easy and good-humoured intonation – it all seems to her to imply a kind of childlike sincerity, as if they all, deep down in their hearts, mean every word they say.

Thus she reasons. And so it is with a light heart and filled with confidence that she now hurries along Porzellangasse to the left, towards Schottenring.

The sun is boiling hot.

The heat seems in fact to increase the closer she gets to the city centre: there is life and movement everywhere, cars hooting, newspaper vendors shouting, and the shop windows enticing with their goods. Down by Berggasse she has to wait several minutes at a crossing. Beside Hörlgasse two nuns are almost run over by a tram. The driver brakes, sticks his head out and begins to scold them but stops short and then bursts out laughing when he sees them eagerly conversing with their veils flapping in the breeze and then continuing over the road as if nothing had happened. An old man in a check jacket shrugs his shoulders and mutters something inaudible. A little girl is playing hopscotch in the corner of Maria Theresien-Strasse.

She continues towards the centre.

And as she believes she is ever closer to the heart of the city, as she thinks she can increasingly clearly discern its rhythm, its regular shifts between still mornings, hot, quicker afternoons and somewhat cooler evenings, spring turns almost imperceptibly into summer: the chestnut trees in Esterhazy Park on Schadekgasse burst into blossom, soon the elder blossom gleams white in parks and in back gardens, and a fine yellow dust is carried on the wind over the city. Then suddenly thundery showers succeed each other, lightning lights up the sky, virginia creeper turns red, it grows gradually darker in the evenings – and before she knows where she is she has already spent almost seven months in the city.

3

My new life! Magda thought, as, just as the clock in St Leopold-skirche struck twelve she went out of the door of the flat in Hockegasse, my new life, she thought and turned the key in the lock. Hesitantly she put the key into her pocket, then went down the two flights of stairs, pushed open the door and went out into the courtyard.

Oh! – she remained standing for a moment and looked around. What pleasantly soft lighting, she thought, and observed the black treetops gleaming with moisture in the heat haze. There was also the mouldering, acid smell of earth, the sonorous sound of the clock that still resonated in the air, tranquillity (only the window of the small tailor's workshop on the ground floor stood ajar as usual; the whirring of a sewing machine could be heard from within).

"What a fine day," she said aloud, half to herself and half to the caretaker who was raking leaves over on the flower beds. The caretaker looked up, glanced up at the greyish white sky and nodded.

"It's mid November," she added as she went passed him, "and yet it's almost ten degrees".

He looked at her and smiled.

"As long as we don't get snow," he called after her when she was already on her way through the flower beds, past the empty benches and the statue of the two white deer. "Everything's fine as long as it doesn't snow."

She laughed quietly to herself. She liked the caretaker, he was always so friendly and helpful. Just as friendly and helpful, she thought, remembering the two jars of dark yellow, sweet plum jam she and Thomas had been given as a housewarming present in September, just as friendly and helpful as his wife. She passed the row of dustbins and hurried through the lower arch out towards Hockgasse. Just as she was about to step out of the darkness of the arch into the pale sunshine of the street she collided with a little boy who came slowly wobbling along on roller skates. "Sorry", she said absentmindedly, wondering if Thomas would nevertheless be late. "Are you all right?" – but by then the little lad had already disappeared.

She crossed over the street down to the tram stop in Gersthofer Strasse, leaned against the plexi glass of the tram shelter and closed her eyes. My new life! she thought again, whilst enjoying the slight warmth of the sun on her eyelids. Or rather: Mein neues Leben. She sampled the words, yes, she thought, just so: what in my own language really has something ludicrous about it, something high flown and pathetic, in this new language has quite a different and much more light-hearted ring to it, a kind of pleasant sweetness – yes, she thought, "mein neues Leben" really sounds just as light and promising as I want it to. Just, she thought at the very moment she heard the tram braking at the tram stop, I suppose just as my life has also come to take shape.

She got on. Went and sat right at the back. Bought a ticket. The compartment was almost empty: apart from herself and the sleepy conductor there were only an elderly couple with a white poodle on their lap and two ten-year-old girls, perhaps sisters – they were dressed in similar brown coats and the same kind of fluffy berets, one light blue, the other red. She looked at them and thought that the words in this new language (which she now thought she mastered rather well) reminded her more than anything of glass marbles – of those transparent glass marbles shot through with thin lines of colour which the girls at school used to play with during break.

It would really be a pity if Thomas was detained at the clinic, she continued. But of course influenza is rife in Ottakring. At that moment the tram swung to the left and braked at Gersthof. An old man with a stick climbed aboard with difficulty and sank down into one of the seats behind the girls. The white poodle jumped up and began to bark but was immediately silenced by a shower of reproaches. I only hope there won't be a case of illness at the last moment, she thought, just as the tram moved off again. Usually she loved to imagine Thomas at work at the clinic, and she was sure that with his energy and optimism he must be an excellent doctor, that the patients must love him. Especially, she thought, the children – and again she saw before her the girls outside the school gate in Glasergasse.

Glass marbles, she thought.

Glass marbles, games, love – and words! Words, it passed through her mind, words which of course if translated back, as it were, have their counterpart in my native tongue, but which for some reason, modesty or pure shame, I would never before have allowed to cross my lips, is it not a fact – and here she cast a quick shy glance around her – that with Thomas now I say things I would never have said previously, indeed is it not a fact that the very phenomenon which the words denote changes character, is transformed in the most remarkable way, when I change languages – so that love itself through this exchange is liberated from the dark and heavy aspects of its being?

Thomas!

She folded her hands in her lap. Among the pedestrians out on the pavement she caught sight of a woman in a blue headscarf. Oh, she thought, just as the tram rounded Aumannplatz and to her surprise she noticed that the little cherry tree in the gardens had lost all its leaves (wasn't is still green only yesterday?) didn't my mother also wear a blue headscarf like that, in fact didn't my mother prefer that very clear sky-blue colour more than any other? Thomas, she thought. Always Café Landtmann. We always have to meet there. Even though there are closer cafés just as good. She laughed quietly to herself. How well she remembered their first meeting, then, in May, only six months ago: she had sat just there in the Café Landtmann flicking through that day's *Neuer Kurier* when, suddenly, she was aware of his presence, had looked up from the newspaper and met his eye, indeed it was there at the Café Landtmann that for the first time she had looked into those light, pale-blue eyes which then, she seemed to remember, had appeared to her both so strange and so familiar, simultaneously intensely present and strangely cold. And immediately afterwards (while trying to think who it was he actually resembled), when she had bent over her newspaper again and pretended to be absorbed in the review of *The Diary of Anne Frank* at the Theater in der Josefstadt on which shortly before she had bestowed very abstracted interest (she remembered this particularly well because they had been at the performance together the following evening) he had asked if he might sit down at her table.

That was really just how it had happened, she thought.

They had remained sitting at the café the whole afternoon. She remembered that he had talked a lot, almost incessantly – about what, on the other hand, she could no longer remember. Perhaps he had told her something about his work at the General Hospital, the Allgemeines Krankenhaus, about how he preferred the mountains and panoramic views to the confinement of the forest and about how he had always dreamt about gliding, perhaps about his family too. Yes, certainly, she thought, he had told her with that mixture of admiration and ill-concealed distaste so typical of him something about his father and his brothers, about his aunt's meddlesomeness and his mother's mild but preoccupied cares (it was actually only a long time later that she realized that his mother had already died when he was ten years old). He had definitely talked about his mother, just as he had about his uncle – the visits he had made as a child together with his Uncle Karl to this very café, the Café Landtmann, belonged to his favourite memories, indeed how many times had she heard him mention how his hunch-backed uncle used to take him there every Sunday, always him and never either of his two brothers, how the uncle, even if on other occasions he could be bewilderingly absent-minded, during the hour which the visit to the café lasted, always appeared to be the most attentive and sensitive listener, how these visits to Café Landtmann therefore constituted the rarest, most precious moments and how he, Thomas, always had to smile at the thought of how his well combed, extravagantly dressed uncle whose chin barely reached above the edge of the table, observed him with a kindly ironic eye, well aware that his little nephew despised himself there at the café for being more ashamed than usual of his uncle's deformity, while simultaneously being proud of how deferentially nevertheless his uncle was treated, was happy to be alone with him and with eager anticipation looked forward to the imminent moment when he would sink his teeth into the portion of Sachertorte and let the apricot jam and dark, bittersweet chocolate slowly melt in his mouth.

Yes, she thought and smiled to herself, while deciding that the two girls were no doubt not only sisters but twins even, so alike they were with their hats, dark hair and small straight noses, Thomas had, on that first instance at Café Landtmann, talked almost incessantly. But then she also remembered suddenly how he had on several occasions stopped in the middle of a sentence, how he had suddenly gone silent and looked at her, curiously, searchingly, almost, she thought, with something resembling fear in his eyes. Yes, she thought, he was surely troubled already then, already there at Café Landtmann, about what he usually calls my "disquieting silence". He had surely already then seized her hands, explained to her that it wasn't only harmful but positively dangerous to allow oneself to be poisoned by the past and appealed to her to deal only with the present. But they aren't just twins, it occurred to her at that moment, when she saw one of the girls whisper something in her sister's ear, they have also grown up in the securest of families and they are very happy.

Forget? she then thought. But isn't that just what I have done?

No doubt it was really only that letter from Sweden (with the photograph which she immediately popped back into the envelope, and with that clause which her eye immediately lighted upon: "…that he has already forgotten all his Hungarian", it was really only the letter that could still make itself felt, the letter, a few isolated words in the crowd on a street, a line in a newspaper – those moments of sudden giddiness before the present took over again. And after that? she thought vaguely whilst the tram clanked past the Volksoper and continued down Währinger Strasse towards the Spitalgasse tram stop. After that..? she again thought just as the tram screeched to a halt. Half a school class climbed aboard. At the stop at the corner of Sensengasse a further ten people got on. "It's true," said a young man, pushing past in the centre aisle, "I saw it with my own eyes". Ah, she thought rather vaguely, Café Landtmann! Café Landtmann, and then, if not on that same evening in any case on one of the following evenings: Theater in der Josefstadt. Thomas! Had it not struck her already then that Thomas was surely one of the most physically tactile people she had ever met, so physical, and that this physical quality had really less to do with his constitution, with the fact that he was quite short and thickset, compact, as it were, and yet remarkably supple, less to do with muscles, sinews, complexion than with something different.

With something light.

Something light and very strong.

Yes, she thought, whilst noticing to her surprise that the couple with the white poodle had disappeared in the direction of the Anatomy Department. Perhaps the very same evening, she thought, and remembered how (although it could equally well have been on another later occasion) they had passed one of the bridges over the canal. For some inexplicable reason she had just asked Thomas precisely when he had seen a dead person for the first time; the air had been mild, the sky deep blue, there had been a cool damp breeze from the canal. Thomas, instead of replying, had put an arm round her waist, pointed over the dirty brown water of the canal and wondered if she too thought the town was at its most beautiful like this in the twilight, his hand had brushed against her hip, she had felt a charge of anticipation and she had thought, yes, it was just then that she thought that although he talked so much it was as if he had a secret – or else as if he had just realized something, something – he didn't know himself exactly what it was – but which he nevertheless burnt with impatience soon, only not yet, to let her share too. And afterwards...? Well, afterwards, she thought, everything had developed very rapidly: before she knew where she was they were already engaged.

The tram had now reached Schottentor. She got up and let herself be borne by the stream out of the compartment. "I'm sorry," somebody said behind her, she turned round and smiled absentmindedly at the woman in the headscarf already on her way. The twin sisters had also disappeared in the crowd. She crossed the tramlines; far over on the opposite platform a florist had set up his wares, buckets of roses, chrysanthemums and gladioli. Just as she noticed that there were pots of mimosa and yellow freesias the clock in the Votiv church struck the half hour. Half past twelve – she had half an hour before she was to meet Thomas at the Café Landtmann. It was no more than a five-minute walk to the café from here. Why had she always got to be in such good time! She stood indecisively for a brief moment beside the cycle crossing, just where the avenue began. She always imagined that the journey would take much longer than it actually did! It is, she thought, as if I was sure that something unpleasant would occur during the journey, something completely unforeseen – and that the resultant delay would in its turn have the most unimagined, indeed almost catastrophic, consequences. How ludicrous, she thought, and took a deep breath. How incredibly stupid! But all the same she had nothing against having time to spare, she liked strolling around the city, she particularly liked the parks – and she decided to walk over to Volksgarten. Admittedly the sun had just disappeared behind a cloud, but it was still just as mild, the smell from the fallen leaves was so fresh and naturally Thomas was right. "You must arrange to go out" that was what he usually said when leaving nowadays, as early in the morning he hurried off to work at the clinic. She knew that he was afraid she would have too much time to think if she stayed at home, morbidly brooding, and no doubt that was why he always left out books which he considered she ought to read, why soon after the move to Hockegasse he had asked to have not his mother's baby grand which was too awkward but her upright piano ("you know of course that my mother was a concert pianist in her youth") and why he was always supplying her with new sheet music (but so far nothing by Liszt), indeed, she thought, perhaps that is why, out of consideration, that he more and more often arranged to meet her in the centre.

At Café Landtmann. Always at Café Landtmann, she thought.

She took the road that followed the cycle path in the avenue. "You should ride out to Nussdorf," he also used to say. "You know that you're always welcome there." And she knew that, naturally. Naturally she ought to take the tram out to Nussdorf, it didn't take more than an hour at the most to get there, naturally Thomas was right – nevertheless, for some incomprehensible reason she had never been able to visit Thomas's family without his company. Even though it was beautiful out there, it really was. And her memories of the angular, dark brown house with its leaded windows, its peculiar small turrets and its leafy garden were all very bright, and of course she remembered summer especially well, the shimmering heat, the smells, all the afternoons and evenings that they had spent in the cool drawing-room on the first floor or on the lawn, in the shade of the apple trees, Ah, in her mind's eye she could recall at any time the picture of the white garden table round which they gathered, Thomas's father and aunt, his eldest brother Stefan (whose piercing eyes always made her feel slightly uncomfortable), his younger brother Martin with his wife Elise and his mandolin, Thomas, herself and, on the very odd occasion, the hunch-backed Uncle Karl. At any time she could see the tray with glasses, the round pale green carafe of wine, the shadow of the foliage on the grass, the vines and rows of resplendent dark roses a little further off. She could see the two children dozing in the white tree hammock, pale freckly little Erich and Elisabeth with her shiny marzipan cheeks and drooping blue rosette, she could see how Elisabeth with the point of her white shoe made the hammock move slightly, so little as to be almost imperceptible, and how the air beyond the hammock in the sunlit hollow on the other side of the house shimmered in the heat.

She crossed the open square in front of the Burgtheater.

And the conversation! she thought. Yes, she remembered many of the summer conversations surprisingly well, some of them almost in detail. Especially those that touched upon Hungary, naturally. Indignant conversations with everybody talking at once, well, she thought, not everybody, not herself since she never really knew what to say, and not Thomas either, really, no, as she remembered it all three brothers had been silent and looked troubled, with the possible exception of Martin. What she remembered all the more clearly was the horror and

71

abhorrence with which the father, aunt and uncle, those immaculately light-clad figures at the other side of the garden table took offence at something that had happened in Hungary only recently, at how as well as the borders with Austria (far into our territory, moreover) now the borders with Yugoslavia had been mined, at how the Hungarian police had captured a refugee who was already in Burgenland and how Kádár only a few days ago had signed an agreement under the terms of which the Soviet troops could remain in the country as long as Moscow wanted.

They had also talked about the budding anti-Semitism in the country.

"In Kádár's Hungary anti-Semitism has become an increasing problem," Thomas's father had declared, leaning back in the garden chair and pressing his finger tips together.

"Obviously," the uncle had interpolated.

The aunt too had nodded in agreement. Then all three (whilst Thomas and Stefan had distractedly twirled their glasses and Martin had bent down for his mandolin) had agreed that the explanation was to be found most of all in the hatred of the Soviet invaders, for, as the father said, ever since the October Revolution most Communists had been Jews and this was also the case with those who now were in power, at least many of them, indeed in actual fact, he was convinced that Kádár inflamed these anti-Semitic tendencies thus to do away with the undesirable elements in his own government.

Whilst crossing over Löwestrasse towards Volksgarten she now imagined she could once again feel the oppressive heat, smell the scent of roses and cigarette smoke. She thought she could also hear the hens cackling on the other side of the fence and see the sugar melt on the apple doughnuts which the aunt has just carried out into the garden. And she remembered her confusion: how strange it was to hear all these names of Hungarian politicians and counter-revolutionaries, of towns, streets and football teams, distorted in the mouths of Thomas's

relatives, how difficult it had been for her to recognize things in
their descriptions (of the political life, but also of the everyday
life they obviously knew about in detail) and how in fact these
descriptions didn't tally at all with the experiences she herself
had had – but how she nevertheless nodded at everything they
said, had smiled in agreement, and how she, despite her slight
surprise, felt something that most of all resembled gratitude. As
if with their words they were offering her a chance to become
one of them, which of course she so very much wanted – but also
as if their pictures, their interpretations and assertions in some
way caused her own memories to fade. Yes, she now thought, it
was really as if during those hot and beautiful days her past had
been transformed into a diffuse and rapidly fading dream.

The father, aunt and uncle had also deplored the fact that the
world had failed its responsibility. Whilst Thomas, Stefan and
Martin exchanged quick glances (of understanding, she now
thought, but what was it they were actually agreed upon?) they
had adjudged that nowadays it was only the Austrians themselves who truly realized the extent of the tragedy that had been
played out and was still being played out at the heart of Europe,
who saw the net being drawn ever tighter and who were indignant at the executions of young people, above all students,
which were of course still taking place in Budapest. "No," the
father said, "not even those who have fled" – and here he nodded kindly towards her, Magda – "no, not even those who have
fled are given help any longer by the rest of the world!" This, he
declared further, was demonstrated by the hunger strike which
had just been carried out in the camps in Siesenheim and
Traiskirchen, a protest which, something the refugees had been
careful to point out, was not in any sense directed against the
country where they have been received but against the rest of
the world, especially America. And which would not have been
called off if the celebrated Frau Roosevelt had not been at one
of the camps herself and promised the hunger strikers she

would do everything in her power to set the American immigration authorities right. Yes, the father, aunt and uncle felt deeply saddened by the world's betrayal, by the fact that Hammarskjöld had made the terrible mistake of stating in the UN quite recently that Kádár ought to be left in peace in his attempts at creating order in his country and similarly by the International Athletics Association's equally fatal mistake of accepting Hungary as a fully fledged member, for naturally, as they had always maintained, sport, in this case football was ultimately a political matter. "And yet just imagine," the aunt had said with a shudder, "only three years ago it still wasn't certain whether Austria would be able to remain a united country. For, only three years ago we still didn't know whether Vienna, just like Berlin, would become a partitioned city or not."

"Dear little friend," she had then said, and leant across the table – Magda could still feel the touch of her hand against her cheek and the faint smell of eau-de-cologne.

And similarly again she felt confusion.

"And the football match to be played in Vienna next week?" Stefan had asked in a quiet, almost indifferent voice.

"And von Karajan?" Thomas added (von Karajan she knew was not only a very old bone of contention between Thomas and his father – von Karajan's membership of the Nazi party was in actual fact the only thing they ever argued about).

There was silence for a moment round the table. The heat was suddenly more oppressive than ever, not a leaf stirred in the foliage above their heads. Martin cleared his throat, cast a quick glance at Thomas, and then asked his father what he thought about von Karajan's choice of repertoire in Seville and whether he had heard anything new about the both magnificent ("there was no denying that after all") and much-needed opera house in Salzburg. "The building's a scandal!", Thomas interrupted. "A 110 million schilling when masses of people have no roof over their heads."

The father was silent.

Uncle Karl stretched up a hand and snatched another one of the sticky apple doughnuts. Martin called to the children to be careful on the hammock. The aunt, on the other hand, looked amused, she coughed discreetly, wiped her lips with the white linen napkin, smiled brilliantly towards the sunlit hollow and declared that she now simply must know what the others thought about something the whole of Vienna was presently talking about: the sex killer from Steyr, "In my opinion a terrible person," she said. "His confession ran to thirty-five pages, and it contains the most gruesome details about how the murders were done. And to think that he has three children and a fourth on the way. A veritable Moosbrugger, that's what he is. Mad, perhaps – but, above all, evil."

"Alfred Engleder," she said. "Alfred Engleder represents nothing less than evil itself."

Then, in fact as far as Magda could remember, not until then, did Elise for the first time begin to say something:

"Engleder hates women," she had said, her bottom lip trembling, with indignation or perhaps sympathy. "He maintains they reject him because he's a dwarf."

A dwarf, Magda thought and now she had reached Volksgarten. She went through the gate, turned left past the beds of labelled roses, away towards the long row of empty green chairs.

Dwarf? she thought, preoccupied, while dusting one of the middle seats with the edge of her coat. And instead of the sex killer from Steyr she saw before her Thomas's uncle, which was naturally grossly unfair. Uncle Karl, Thomas always used to say, is the best and most honourable man I've ever known, in fact if anything, he used to say, Uncle Karl is too good, almost idiotically kind-hearted, a judgement, she was sure, that alluded to events during the war years, events which she really knew little about but which she suspected were connected with his role as a cripple. "No, Uncle Karl", Thomas used to say, "is never sorry for himself and he's always equally benignly appreciative towards everybody around him". Appreciative! The word shot up towards the surface of her conscious mind, flashed and disappeared again – leaving behind a translucent picture of Thomas's father. How strange! she thought. It's usually Thomas who maintains that he can never think of his Uncle Karl without a picture of his father with his pale complexion, his white hair combed back, his round, steel-rimmed spectacles and his narrow lips (yes, she thought, they really were narrow) slipping in between. How different Thomas always is in his father's presence, she continued to muse, so well-mannered and at the same time so strangely remote, almost, she thought, as if the pointer of his inner magnet had gone out of order and started to quiver as soon as his father approached – and now she suddenly heard the particular, almost silent note in Thomas's voice when, almost always with a slight laugh, he talked about his father's distinction, his father's successes in world of education, his musicality, his talents as a rose breeder and his bloodhound sense of smell. "He always firmly maintained that when he'd been occupied elsewhere he could who'd been looking for him in his headmaster's office by the smell", Thomas used to say. "This thoroughly admirable father", as he'd also said more or less, "whom nevertheless I've never been able to make myself touch, let alone embrace, and concerning whom it's impossible to decide whether his ardent passion for roses and all sorts of art is an expression of spirituality or a childish need to, well, an almost unhealthy desire to impress". Oh, she thought at that moment and let her gaze sweep over the extensive flower beds before her, oh, how fresh the roses still look! Just a slight browning at the edges. And the air is so gentle! Everything gleams so beautifully with moisture and dampness! Yes, surely, she continued, everything will turn out for the best, just as it did with the flat (it had been a pure miracle that they had got hold of a flat so close to the hospital), surely, she thought, I shall find a new job very soon – if not at the school in Glasergasse then somewhere else!

An old man approached the seat where she was sitting. He walked with his eyes on the ground, slowly, and cautiously groping forward with his stick. He was bare-headed, his sparse white hair moved slightly in the light breeze, he seemed to be deep in his own thoughts, indeed he seemed completely unaware that she was sitting only a few yards away, unaware of the little girl in a black coat skipping over by the gate, of the dogs playing on the grass, of the roses, the grey mist and the distant clanking of the tram. Just as he was passing her seat, though, he did turn and cast a hasty, piercing glance at her – before continuing his cautious wandering towards the exit. "It' s got colder," she heard him murmur (whether to her or mostly to himself was impossible to decide). "It won't be long before we get snow."

The next moment he was gone.

Snow? She repeated the word silently to herself.

Oh, she thought, of course!

And she suddenly felt a desire to laugh out loud in delight.

Of course, she thought happily, of course it will soon start to snow.

1963

1

"She's called Margaretha", Thomas had said, "she's seven, her parents said they could envisage two lessons a week and they want her to start by Monday."

"Isn't it fantastic!" he had also said. "Since you've been out of work so long.

"Once you've got one pupil you'll soon get more."

And he had looked at her with his light, enquiring eyes. "Aren't you pleased?"

She had replied that of course she was very pleased. And grateful. To him, for having taken so much trouble, and to his aunt who had been kind enough to use her connections. For of course, even if private pupils were very different from working at a school it was always a start. After which she had sat down at the piano and played for him. She had intended to play a piece by Brahms which she knew that he loved, but then, really without any reason, she had changed her mind and played the quite unknown work by Liszt that she had just learnt and that she knew that he hadn't heard before. Ever since the day the piano had been heaved upstairs, placed against the short wall of the living-room right opposite the balcony, she had loved to have him as her audience; the knowledge that he was listening always filled her with tenderness and anticipation – but this time, yesterday afternoon, when she had played the rather sentimental Lizst ballade for him she had suddenly also felt something else, a kind of defiance, a childish desire to – well, what? Burst out laughing? Or start to cry, savagely and unrestrained?

But when she had played the piece to the end and turned round to receive his applause she had to her surprise found him silent and introspective. He had sat there, on the chair in front of the balcony, with an unlit cigarette dangling between his thumb and index finger and with his gaze lost in the distance, and with a flash of insight she had known that he was thinking about the child, not the unknown Margaretha who would be making her entrance here in only a few days' time, but their own child which he longed for so intensely but which she with the same intensity refused to bring into the world.

"What did you think?" she had asked.

Then he had given a start and looked at her as if woken from sleep. Thereupon he had smiled slightly and bent over the table for the matches.

Behind his back the snow had fallen heavily.

In fact it had snowed incessantly for more than a week, and although the snowploughs had been working round the clock in an attempt to keep the streets more or less passable and although thousands of road workers had done their best to keep the tramlines free from snow and ice, chaos still reigned in the town. Enormous snowdrifts blocked the pavements. Those cars which still dared to go out, and there were surprisingly many, skidded over the roads and got stuck now and then in the drifts. Only a few trams could get through at all. For the whole of last week, it had been at least minus ten degrees as well, there was a cruel wind and even if, just as she had hurried the short distance from the tram stop on Schottentor, it had cleared up a little, it was impossible to stay outside for any length of time.

But when chilled to the bone and with her heart in her mouth, she had gone through the door of Café Landtmann it was not relief that she felt, not satisfaction at finally being indoors – at the very moment she entered the café's sweetish damp warmth she was overwhelmed (why? she was to wonder later, why just then?) by a momentary faintness, by a sudden and so strong a rush of unpleasantness that she immediately regretted that she and Thomas had arranged to meet just here, just here at Café Landtmann, and when she soon realized into the bargain that Thomas was delayed she was seized with an immediate and equally strong impulse to turn and run: to hurry back out into the cold, take the very first tram home (if there was one to take) and pretend that she had forgotten the arranged meeting. But while she was still hesitating, standing irresolutely at the counter, a waiter appeared. Suddenly he was simply standing there, between her and the exit, with his inscrutable gaze fixed on a point immediately above her left ear and pointing towards the vacant table in the centre of the room to the left, with an expression both disdainful and regretful so it seemed to her.

She grew confused. Wanted to say something. Perhaps explain herself.

Before she could utter a word, however, they were already on their way through the crowded rooms, steering between the tables, newspaper rack and projecting palm leaves, he in front, skilfully balancing on the fingers of one hand his silver tray with a glass of water, and she behind, with mounting reluctance, in fact suspicion, observing his black back, broad neck and blond hair combed as carefully as ever across his bald pate — and when he immediately afterwards pulled out the chair for her she imagined that really he knew very well not only that Thomas was delayed, but also why.

She tried to banish the thought.

When he remained, however, when he brushed a few non-existent crumbs off the tablecloth and then, without a word, placed not one but two glasses in front of her on the table, she was certain that he was concealing something from her. That he was deliberately silent, that his silence gave him a feeling of advantage – and that he was enjoying it, as well.

The next moment, before she herself had had time to ask anything, he was gone.

To her surprise she felt her heart pounding strongly in her breast, felt that her mouth was dry and her skin was drawn tightly over her cheeks in a strange way. She also noticed that she was sitting holding her back as straight as a ramrod and that she was clenching her hands so tightly in her lap that her knuckles had gone white.

She tried to relax.

She struggled to breathe normally and to stop trembling. She took off her coat, folded it carefully and laid it on the chair beside her, tidied her hair, passed her tongue over her dry lips and drank a little water.

Then she looked around.

Only now did she notice that from here, from this table in the middle of the room (the most exposed place and therefore one she had avoided earlier) she had a view looking on to the Burgtheater and Ringen. Straight ahead she could see a newspaper vendor's coat shining bright yellow against the snow which had piled up against the theatre's stone wall, if she turned her head just a fraction to the right she could see how the branches of the plane trees stood out against the pale sky, two men busy digging a blue car out of the snow drifts and a little girl in a black coat cautiously poking the snow with the toe of her shoe.

A pale sun now shone through the café's tall windows.

Slowly the warmth began to spread throughout her body. After a while she leant back in her chair. She closed her eyes. And while she now listened to the hum of voices which rose and fell around her she felt that she was really very tired. Finally a pleasant drowsiness spread over her, a feeling of relief, of peace.

Perhaps she even fell asleep.

Then, out of the light resistance of her nap an image arose, in a flash, unexpected and with a definition that made her give a start and quickly open her eyes again: the long row of darkly dressed girls, of well wrapped up young figures with similar dirty yellow hair rosettes swaying like slightly overblown water-lilies on the backs of their coats.

The girls! shot through her mind. Their tiredness! Tiredness and – trust, the childlike and terrifying trust with which they trudged along the narrow wild track over the mountain!

Over the mountain and over the border.

She passed her hand over her eyes.

Oh, now there were other images too: the translucent blue sky, the ground covered with a thin layer of snow, the surrounding mountains gleaming so unnaturally white in the afternoon sun. There was the stream down in the hollow, black and smooth as if its surface had been covered with a thin layer of hardened lacquer. There were the abandoned watchtowers. The half-bare hazel bushes. The withered grass swaying in the slight, icy wind. Far ahead a glimpse of some red and white flags.

Then: somebody who turns round. Who waves, laughs – but everything happens quietly and silently as in a dream.

It was Dóra, she thought, it was Dóra who went first. "What if the path (wasn't that what she had said ?) despite the farmers' assurances has been mined all the same."

She herself of course had gone last. With the boy by the hand.

József – and at that moment, very briefly and for the first time for as long as she could remember, she caught a glimpse of his face.

Then she hastily stretched out her hand, seized the glass of water, raised it to her lips and simultaneously let her eye sweep over the room – but no, nobody seemed to have noticed anything. Everything seemed calm. A subdued hum could be heard from the inner room, out here where she sat a sleepy silence reigned, the old man at the table beside hers turned the page of his newspaper, very carefully and so slowly that it could hardly be heard.

Then she breathed out.

But just as she was about to put the glass down she gave such a start that the water spilled over and formed a pale grey stain on the white table cloth: the waiter was standing right behind her, so close in fact that his elbow almost touched her shoulder!

How long had he been standing there? Had he spoken to her? Had he murmured something she hadn't heard?

She looked up at him, enquiringly, uncertain – but instead of repeating his words, if in fact he had said anything, he turned to the old man at the next table. "It's a disgrace," muttered the old man behind his newspaper. "We shall all be without water." And the waiter agreed that the situation was catastrophic. That everybody must help to save it, not least households, but that – and here he bent over and pointed at the paper – people's dislike of obeying orders had already had consequences: "in many parts of the town the hot water boilers have become unusable".

Then he was gone again.

She suddenly felt close to tears.

A school excursion? she thought in despair. Was that really what we'd said to the girls?

A Sunday excursion up into the mountains?

Did they really know nothing? Did they really still believe, as they trudged along the path over the mountain, that they would be returning home towards evening?

And where are they now?

József, she thought again. József!

Then – by chance?- she met the old man's eye over the corner of his newspaper. Just very briefly, before he quickly disappeared behind the paper again.

And that mental image? she thought. The image of the girls? Why does it seem all at once so impenetrable? Why does it seem to me, she thought, as with a pounding heart she bent over her handbag and opened it, only to close it again straight away, why does it seem to me as if the very moment we crossed the border all that was fantastic, wonderful, magnificent which surely must have been there – the valley which opened out below us, the sunspots, the dark blue shadows, the sudden, giddy feeling of absolute weightlessness – had really never existed.

She reached out her hand again for the glass, took a few gulps – but the water had got warm and acquired a cloying aftertaste which immediately made her feel sick. She had a fit of trembling, almost like ague – and again she had to look around her quickly. The other guests didn't seem to have noticed anything now either, however, no, everybody around her still seemed to be occupied with their own business, reading the newspaper, chatting or taking up their cake with their fork.

Whence then this sudden fear, almost panic?

Perhaps she ought to order something anyway? Perhaps she ought to ask for her usual *Einspänner* even though Thomas hadn't arrived? She waved to the waiter – but regretted it as soon as he came up to her table. No, no, she didn't want anything! He bowed and disappeared without a word.

Cold sweat now broke out on her brow. And she was suddenly certain – the old man at the neighbouring table had noted her indecision. But that wasn't all. He hadn't only noticed it – he also found it peculiar!

Her thoughts reeled, she tried desperately to fasten her gaze on the grey façade of the Burgtheater.

Can one…? She forced herself to think.

Have I…?

And then: Is it Tuesday of next week Thomas and I are invited to Martin's?

Or is it on Sunday?

And how can little Erich be really so unlike his father? Erich, with his great head, his milk-white skin and his strangely slow moments.

Martin is dark after all.

And that business about his being so awfully fat as a child is surely not true.

Yes of course! Erich's birthday is on Tuesday.

So we really ought to be buying him a present today.

Perhaps a baseball bat? Unless he's too little for that. In that case a toy animal of some sort – why not a paper kite?

A green paper kite with black wings?

If you can buy paper kites in the autumn, that is.

When Thomas comes, she thought, I shall ask his advice.

If he comes, that is! Confused she glanced at the clock: five minutes past two. Thomas was therefore over an hour late! Why hadn't he rung? If something had come up at the clinic he ought to have rung here as he usually did.

She looked around in panic. She had to get away from here, at once, before everything was too late! She stretched out her hand for her coat. But just as she was about to pull it towards her, her eyes happened to glance once more at the old man at the next table. She saw that he was sitting bent over his newspaper, that his thin white hair moved slightly in the draught from the window and that, when lifting his cup to his mouth, he did so without interrupting his reading for a moment. Even so she could no longer free herself from the impression that something was wrong – from the unpleasant, diffuse feeling that in actual fact he was dissembling. That he, and not only he but the other customers in the café, were only pretending to be occupied with other things, with their newspapers, their table companions or their confections, while for quite some time, as she had suspected all along, they had really been sitting observing her in secret and that it was only now, when they had realized that she was on to them, that they had quickly and all together in complete unison, turned their gaze elsewhere. An icy terror seized her, a horrible, giddy feeling of standing beside an abyss – and the thought of getting up to go, of passing through the café exposed to the gaze of the other customers, was suddenly an impossiblity.

What was she to do now? She suddenly felt as if something in her head was about to burst, as if her heart had swollen and as if her skull, the cranium itself, was on the verge of exploding like the shell of an enormous over-ripe fruit. But then, yes, just then, the yellow jacket of the newspaper vendor appeared in the door of the café. Why now? she thought and noticed at that moment, to her consternation, that with his curly brown hair and his long drooping moustache he actually resembled some-one, someone she had once known. Why just this afternoon? Oh, why had he come just today, she couldn't remember ever having seen him here before! And now: not only did he say something to the waiter, adjust the bag on his shoulder and stroke his moustache, he also began to talk to the customers – indeed while going back and forth between the tables and offer-ing his copies of *Neuer Kurier* for sale, he actually gossiped with them, friendly and familiarly, as if he had really known them all very well for a long time.

And what, she wondered, should she say when he came up to her table?

She didn't want a paper, of course. She couldn't even think of reading today's *Neuer Kurier*, no, especially not the *Neuer Kurier*! But – she suddenly realized – if it hadn't been for the strange business of his appearing just now, and for all the other things, she would have bought a copy nevertheless. She would have bought one without thinking about it, only because – oh, that thought filled her with real horror – only because the oth-ers were doing so. Now, however, she didn't know what to do. But suddenly it was as if just buying the *Neuer Kurier*, that's to say doing it because the others were doing so, and so mostly to be one of them really, would only serve as yet another confir-mation of what everybody in here had already understood: that in actual fact she didn't belong here and, no matter what she tried to imagine, she never would.

No!

And for that very reason she would not buy a newpaper, for that very reason she must not under any circumstances buy a copy of today's *Neuer Kurier*!

Absolutely not!

When the newspaper vendor at that moment was almost up to her table, however, just as he had taken the old man's money, it occurred to her instead – unless it was that her courage had deserted her – that despite everything it would be even more painful to say no to his query than to say yes, and that she emphasized her alienation more by not purchasing a paper than by purchasing one, and that it was after all precisely such an emphasis that she wanted to avoid. Before she had had time to consider any further, therefore, she reached for her handbag, took out a few coins and counted out two schilling into the palm of her hand.

Then she turned and held them out – but only to find to her consternation that the vendor had already gone past her. That he was on his way back to the exit. Indeed, he was about to leave the café without having taken the least bit of notice of her.

As if he hadn't even been aware of her. Or – as if she didn't even exist.

József? she thought panicstricken. József…!

At that moment Thomas was standing there – smilingly he leant over and laid his hand on her shoulder.

She met his gaze, his very light and kindly enquiring gaze – and she knew immediately that she wouldn't tell him about her recent experience. That it would not only be unwise but utterly fatal to let him know about the fear which had overpowered her only a short time ago and which in some incomprehensible way seemed to have threatened her whole existence.

At dawn on the day the first lesson with the girl was to take place Magda was awoken by the church bells slowly penetrating her sleep, for a fraction of a second she imagined she was back in

Sándor's dark little room in Szent Mihály utca, imagined she could almost smell the scent of sweet-smelling stocks in bloom and garbage – then the sound of the bells died away and she became aware of where she was. Aware that Thomas was asleep beside her with his arms above his head, that he was smiling in his sleep and that saliva was gleaming on his lower lip, aware that the silhouette of the bedhead cast a dark shadow on the wallpaper, that the wardrobe door was ajar and that a half-eaten apple lay on the bedside table.

She also had a vague feeling of having dreamt.

But what? There were fragments of darkness and light, of something that could be a backyard, perhaps a street or rather a road – otherwise nothing. She closed her eyes again (recalling the dream seemed to her suddenly to be more important than anything else, indeed it was as if all at once everything depended on it, depended on her succeeding in remembering in detail the course of the dream) – but she soon noticed that the more she struggled to remember the more the dream seemed to evade her, that in actual fact she was groping in a vacuum and that, against her will, she was sinking deeper and deeper into a trance-like state – a heavy, grey-white state more like unconsciousness than sleep.

When she awoke again Thomas had gone.

The clatter of a snowplough could be heard from the street. She got up. The room was cold. It was even colder in the kitchen. Thomas had put a clean cup on the table, the teapot was on the bench, there was water in the saucepan, the gas lighter was laid ready. She rinsed her face in the warm water from the tap, then got dressed, drank a cup of hot tea and ate a slice of bread and plum jam. It was snowing outside. Large, heavy flakes whirled in the air, the crowns of the plane trees gleamed white. The dream, she thought, that street in the dream – isn't it really a memory from my childhood?

The St Leopold church clock struck nine.

Suddenly she was in a hurry: now there were only two hours, she realized suddenly, before the girl was due, and somehow she must prepare herself. Perhaps, she thought, whilst putting the teacup in the sink, perhaps I ought to offer her something? And then I must have some paper to write on, blank manuscript paper, perhaps a few simple notes. She put on her winter boots, coat and gloves, wound a shawl round her head and quickly left the flat. The stationer's in Genzgasse! she thought. They're sure to have what I need.

Out in the courtyard she met the caretaker. He was leaning on his snow shovel looking glumly up at the leaden sky. As she approached he touched his cap, nodded and asked her how she was. "And there's supposed to be more snow," he said in the same breath. "Who knows what will happen with the lottery at the weekend."

She wanted to pass but he held her back.

"I told you, didn't I, about last week's lottery?" he asked conspiratorially and leant his head so far forward that his earflaps almost touched her shoulder. "About the twenty-second week?"

She took a step backwards.

"That too", he chuckled, "was cancelled. The weather in England is almost as awful as here. And now… this time.."

Here he seized her arm with his padded glove.

"This time, the twenty-third, the rolled over jackpot is up to ..to almost …twenty million schilling.

"Do you realize?" he whispered,"do you realize what that means?

"How much you can win?

"Do you realize that on Saturday you could be – a millionaire! A millionaire!" he smiled. "Me – just as well as anybody else".

And he looked at her with a gleaming, half-absent gaze. She wanted to say something, to show that she had understood and that she was impressed – but before she had got out a word he had already turned his back on her and continued with the thankless task of clearing the paths of snow.

At the stationer's in Genzgasse she bought manuscript paper, two notebooks with yellow wax covers, a black ballpoint pen and a sheet of golden stars, in the music shop almost as far as Sensengasse she found two piano tutors for beginners, but when she thought that they both seemed badly presented she decided instead to follow her instinct and selected only the music to a few simple Austrian children's rhymes which she assumed the girl would already recognize, at Café Lintner finally she bought a quarter of chocolate pralines and a small bag of burnt almonds. It was still snowing when she returned to Hockegasse. The caretaker was no longer to be seen, perhaps he had given up for the time being and was waiting for better weather.

She had a quick lunch.

She washed up, made the bed and tidied up the living room. It was almost noon by the time she finally sat down at the carefully cleaned kitchen table to prepare the first lesson. When at the stroke of two, the doorbell rang she was sitting still absorbed in her papers. She gave a start, quickly smoothed her hair with her hand and hurried out into the hall.

With a pounding heart she turned the key in the lock.

And there they stood. A tall, slender lady in a loden coat and Tyrolean hat, with short, dark-blond hair, dark-red lips and dark-red earrings in the shape of roses – and a short and fat little girl with a doughish-white complexion. The girl was wearing a beret and from under the beret protruded two thin, white plaits. She was wearing a grey coat with a belt tied tightly over her round tummy. And she was wearing spectacles with such thick lenses that it was impossible at first glance to decide whether she really saw the person in front of her or if she was observing an invisible point somewhere far away in the distance. "Margaretha!" the lady said, and pushed the girl ahead of her over the threshold. "This is little Margaretha." She then leant over the girl who stood there shy, awkward, her arms hanging stiffly at her sides. "Curtsey nicely!" she said and smiled knowingly at Magda over the girl's head. Only then did she extend a gloved hand. She introduced herself. She explained that she was looking forward to her daughter learning to play the piano, that the girl was shy but willing to learn and that it would suit her herself best if the lessons could take place every Monday and Friday between two and three in the afternoon. She emphasized the importance of little Margaretha finding her own way in future from their villa in Naaffgasse here to Hockegasse, a walk of at most fifteen minutes which would give the girl both necessary exercise and increased self-confidence. She talked, she smiled with white teeth, and whilst helping the girl off with her outdoor clothes, straightening her plaits, taking off her spectacles and drying them with her handkerchief and putting them back on again she looked around in the hall with such abstracted attention that it was impossible to decide whether her thoughts were already somewhere else or if Magda, the hall and the visible part of the living-room were being subjected to a thorough and inquisitive inspection. She would return at three o'clock to fetch her daughter, she finally explained, "but then only on this one occasion". She patted the girl lightly on the cheek, smiled at Magda and gave one final quick look around her.

And then she was gone.

Magda took little Margaretha by the hand and led her into the living room. Since the girl still looked terrified she began by offering her a chocolate praline. Then she placed her on the oblong piano stool and sat down beside her. They were now sitting so close to each other that she could feel the warmth exuding from the girl's body and the vague but unmistakable smell of cheap soap, like the slight smell of – well, what? Submissiveness? Fear? Perhaps, which was even more disturbing, pure shame? It now transpired that the girl was completely ignorant of anything connected with music, even the simplest principles, and what was worse, she had short, round and stiff fingers with which it was almost impossible to play.

"May I see your hand," Magda asked.

She took the girl's left hand carefully and put it in hers. And whilst closely inspecting the hand, whilst turning it and letting her fingertips glide carefully over all the small dimples, over the really very short and very chubby fingers and over the soft doughy-white skin of the palm she felt a wave of tenderness well up inside her, indeed the sight of this hand, like everything else about this awkward, clumsy and defenceless child, brought tears of pity to her eyes.

"And now the other one," she asked – and resolved at once to do everything in her power to win the girl's confidence. She will never learn to play the piano, she thought, at least not within the foreseeable future. But what does that matter, after all? Aloud she said: "You've strong fine hands. Kind hands that have never harmed the tiniest fly."

Little Margaretha stared stubbornly down at her lap. She looked as though she was about to sink through the floor with shame. Magda explained that you needed flexible fingers to play and that the girl should therefore bend and stretch her fingers for a while every morning and evening. "Now first we shall look for a C," she then said. "C is to the left of those two black keys."

They found C and worked out that there were seven Cs on the keyboard. They agreed on how to write C, how one differentiated a minim from a crotchet, and that the note immediately above C was called D, that the one immediately below was B. Then little Margaretha had to play a short melody that covered what she now had learnt.

Magda praised the girl.

She smiled encouragingly at her.

And she asked if there were any composer that Margaretha was especially fond of, she played the first movement of the

Moonlight Sonata for her and promised that given time she herself would be able to play not only that first movement but the
following ones too. Then she offered the girl more chocolates,
handed her the manuscript with the little three-note melody,
encouraged her to practise diligently for the next lesson and
asked how things were at school. To her surprise the girl
answered – she cast a hasty, bashful glance through her thick
lenses, blushed and murmured something about it not being
very nice but that her mummy had said that it would soon be
better.

"It's up to me," she said quietly.

And then she looked at Magda and smiled with lips sticky
with chocolate. Magda handed her her handkerchief.
"Although", the little child continued in the same breath – in a
whisper now where the words could barely be discerned –
"Mummy says my fingers look like little ice cream-cornets."

At that moment the doorbell rang.

That evening Magda told Thomas about the girl's visit. "You
feel you have to be sorry for her," she said. "She gives the
impression of being a very unhappy and very lonely child." She
sat down at the piano. Thomas stood behind her, she caught a
glimpse of him like a shadow in the shining black veneer of the
piano: his dark, barely discernible form, his hands like lighter
patches on her shoulders, his eyes tentatively seeking hers. He
was serious, almost determined, and it was impossible to decide
whether he was listening, in fact whether he had even heard a
word she had said. "A very lonely child," she repeated – and the
hold on her shoulder hardened. For a brief moment his fingers
pressed so hard against her collar-bone that she cried out in
pain. Then his hands immediately released their hold and
began instead to wander upwards caressingly, gliding over her
neck, over her earlobes, cheeks and temples – before in an even
slower and lighter movement searching their way down again,

resting finally on her shoulders once again, more gently now but more expectant too, rather, it occurred to her, like a cat ready to pounce. She held her breath. Waited with her eyes fixed on his hands' light patches in the shining black veneer. The silence between them grew increasingly pregnant. Then he took hold of her head, bent it lightly backwards, leant over her and brought his lips to hers, so slowly that she registered that his breath was dry and hot and that it smelt slightly of garlic. Then he kissed her.

They kissed for a long time. More and more passionately and with a kind of frenzied despair that had never been there before.

That same night she dreamt again about the street – about the street she thought she vaguely recognized from the Budapest of her childhood. When she awoke it was light outside. Now too it made her uneasy that the dream soon faded, that it dispersed and disappeared the moment she opened her eyes and looked around, now too the feeling of unease was strengthened by the fact that Thomas had already had time to leave. She got up, had breakfast and left the flat. It was cold outside, but the sky was clear and a pale winter sun rose slowly over the house tops. The snow lay in waist-high drifts, it was sometimes difficult to make your way along the footpaths. She walked aimlessly, driven by this strange and vague feeling of loss, of desperate impotence, in fact almost fear at the dream having slipped away as soon as she thought she could discern its shape. For several hours she wandered around the district. She went up Hockegasse for a while, turned off to the left, crossed the park by St Leopoldskirche and continued up Bastiengasse. Outside the Semmelweis clinic an ambulance was parked, a woman was just being lifted out on to a stretcher and hurriedly carried through the gate; on the bridge just beyond the clinic an icy wind was blowing. She hurried on upwards. For a short while she lingered at the viewpoint on the Dürwahringstrasse: she glimpsed the houses in the snow-covered valley below like small dark spots, the sky above was now marble-white. For a while she considered continuing out to Naaffgasse to see where little Margaretha lived, but then she changed her mind and walked instead in a wide semi-circle towards the churchyard, changed her mind again, turned, reached the park again beside St Leopoldskirche, stopped and for a long time, for what must surely have been almost half an hour, stood watching the children playing on the snow-covered football field – until, suddenly frozen stiff, she turned about face and almost ran the short distance home.

The days that followed were in some peculiar way lighter than usual. Whilst the nights were still filled with those dark, confused, half-disintegrated dreams (which vanished as soon as she awoke) the days were imbued with the sharp whiteness of the snow, a whiteness that made everything around her stand out more clearly than before, as if from a new and unexpected perspective. On Wednesday she went early in the morning to the library in Neubau to return a book, to the tailor's to fetch Thomas's new winter coat and to the toy shop in Mariahilfer Strasse (but without managing to get a paper kite). In the afternoon she prepared her next piano lesson and sewed a button on her blouse. She also talked to her sister-in-law on the phone, a short and rather confused conversation – she never really understood what it was about. In the evening they had dinner at Thomas's father's. On the way to Canovagasse Thomas told her about his work, he mentioned a strange case of poisoning they had just got at the clinic, and a three-year-old boy who had had a cold continually ever since birth, he fell silent for a brief moment and then lost himself in speculation about what a wonderful science immunology was: what it studied really encompassed the necessary conditions for life itself. He smiled, he gesticulated, and while with a far-seeing look he expatiated on the fact that the concentrations of salt, sodium potassium and chlorides in every human being's blood, just as cobalt, magnesium and zinc in her tapestries, were precisely the same as those already in the young oceans millions of years ago, he took her hand, put it to his lips and kissed it. Then he laughed, pointed at the illuminated façade of the Volksoper and mentioned, as if in passing, something about his Uncle Karl having always been a passionate admirer of Austrian youth and that "when I myself was a child he always treated me as an equal – which was naturally made easier by my uncle, with the enormous hunch on his back, being shorter in height than even the smallest ten-year-old." She looked at him out of the corner of her eye: the light eyelashes, the powerful jaw, the straight line of the upper lip. Now, she thought and at the same time heard deep down inside her head some short, disconnected notes from Liszt's *Missa choralis*, now he'll soon start to talk about his father. But he didn't. In actual fact he was silent after his remarks about his uncle right up until they got off at Schottentor ("Are you cold?" he then wondered. "Would you mind walking the rest of the way?"), in fact it wasn't really until several hours later on the way home again that he took up where he had left off, but not even then to talk about his father but to praise yet again the science to which he wanted to devote his future – whilst the tram rattled towards Gersthof he involved himself in a description of the experiment with white blood corpuscles that the students had had to carry out that same afternoon, a detailed description of how they had had to extract granulocytes from ten cubic centimetres of blood, place them in a bowl of salt water and see how they reacted when a single bacterium was added. "Ah, that's it," he exclaimed just as the tram pulled up at the tramstop, "the ability to distinguish beween one's own and alien species has really been wholly decisive for the survival of the human body." And all the way from the tram stop, across the street, across the snow-covered courtyard and up all the stairs he continued with mounting enthusiasm to elaborate on the mystery of the white corpuscles and on the granulocytes as the result of a never-ending development, "a development that had not only favoured those who had possessed the greatest ability to provide sustenance but at the same time those who had been most aggressive and who had been best at defending themselves".

The *Missa choralis*? she thought. Why just the *Missa choralis*?

She spent Thursday reading. Now and then she let the book sink down on to her lap so as instead to observe the various objects in the room, all those things around her that in the different and somehow brighter light which now prevailed, seemed to stand out with such surprising clarity: the candelabra on the piano, the armchair with its purple seat, the sofa, the grandfather clock, the chest of drawers and the thin white curtains. She also prepared the lesson for the next day. Ate some fruit. Had a cup of tea. And it struck her suddenly, just as she sat down at the piano, that nobody in her surroundings here, not even Thomas really, knew that in fact she had never studied music, that Hungarian had been her only teaching subject before and that it was Sándor who had taught her to play.

Twice during the day she found an excuse for going out.

First to the postbox, with one of those customary and, so it might seem (she had not received a single reply in four years) completely useless enquiries about vacant appointments, in this case, as so often before, at the school in Glasergasse.

Then to the dustbins.

On both occasions she met the caretaker, on both occasions he had stopped his work, rested his arms on the snow shovel and leant so far forward towards her that she could smell his breath – and on both occasions he asked her in whispering tones what she, just she, thought about this coming Saturday's lottery.

Little Margaretha arrived in good time before two o'clock. She stood there just inside the doorway, her ears blood-red from the cold, with her beret pulled down over her forehead and with icy, completely steamed-up spectacles. She was holding a brown paper bag in front of her like a shield in her outstretched hand and she seemed almost as terrified as the first time.

But she smiled.

Yes, she really smiled, a very uncertain and barely perceptible smile. Magda accepted the bag and opened it – there lay a small bunch of grapes wrapped in a paper napkin. From whom? she thought. From Margaretha or from her mother? She thanked her. Then she helped the little girl off with her coat, wiped her spectacles clean and led her to the piano in the living room.

The hour at their disposal vanished almost without their noticing it.

Margaretha performed her very short and very simple three-note melody with some difficulty: she got stuck again and again in the middle, grew hotter and unhappier, and didn't calm down until Magda laughingly stated that the passage wasn't all that easy and helped her by carefully guiding her fingers over the keys. Then they found E and A, together they wrote a G-clef, and an F-clef and a repeat symbol and listened to the difference between two-four and three-four time. Margaretha was eager to learn, she followed everything attentively and glowed with delight every time she got something right. On this occasion too Magda played a piece by Beethoven for her, and again promised that the girl in time would be able to play something similar herself. Then she rose and went to get the chocolates.

By this time Margaretha's cheeks glowed with excitement. The girl took a chocolate. She munched, slowly and with a strangely brooding expression written all over her little round face. Between chews she interrupted her cogitations now and again, looked up at Magda and smiled – a smile that was no longer frightened but open and filled with confidence. It was already almost half-past three when they got up and went out into the hall. Magda helped Margaretha on with her coat. She tied the belt round her plump tummy and adjusted the beret on her head.

Just as Margaretha was about to go, indeed she had already curtseyed and was standing with one hand on the door knob, she turned round and declared that the worst thing about school wasn't that she was teased but that she was never left in peace during the breaks.

"I don't want to talk to anybody," she said.

Then Magda bent down, put her arms around her and kissed her on the cheek.

On Monday she took out the gold stars. They appeared to have a devastating effect – when little Margaretha caught sight of them she burst into tears. Then she smiled and her eyes behind the thick spectacle lenses began to sparkle. And when, after the girl had played the piece set for the day's lesson with the same difficulty as the first time, Magda stuck a star, one of the smaller ones, on to page three in her book, a deep sigh emerged from the little girl's breast – a sigh so filled with enthusiasm and at the same time so exhausted that Magda immediately promised herself that from now on, after every lesson, she would stick on a new one – however the playing developed and no matter whether or not the girl made any progress.

And so it was, too.

And not only one star but often two, on occasion even three. Large and small indiscriminately.

This little ceremony, which after every performance was carried out in devout silence, seemed each time not only to fill little Margaretha with ever-increasing anticipation and gratitude – it also seemed to amuse Magda more and more.

Until one day she made an unexpected discovery: when after the seventh or eighth lesson she flicked through the yellow book she was suddenly seized, at the sight of all these stars, with the most peculiar and contradictory emotions – and she had to ask herself what this whole parade of semi-constellations, so to speak, had come to symbolize. If they any longer at all marked little Margaretha's progress in piano-playing (progress which was admittedly modest but was all the same not so wholly non-existent as she herself had predicted), or instead the change the girl's personality had undergone or, in a kind of inverted perspective, all the sad and pitiful things she had by this time got to know about her life.

Yes, Magda thought in dismay, that's just it.

With every lesson they had had Margaretha had grown calmer, increasingly confident – but also increasingly outspoken. She always arrived shortly before two o'clock, always panting eagerly, always with steamed-up spectacles and always holding her little brown bag in front of her, and except for the half-hour when she played the piece for that day or listened to the piece for the next lesson and when she really concentrated hard, she talked incessantly – and now about everything. Not only about school, about her tormentors in the higher classes and her dread of gym lessons, but also about how things were at home, about her constant gnawing hunger and about how she despised herself for being so fat and so completely different from her beautiful mother. But mostly, Magda thought, although she doesn't call it that: about her loneliness.

In fact the greater the insight she had gained during these weeks into little Margaretha's life the more dismayed she had become – and the stronger her sympathy grew. In her mind's eye she saw increasingly often the enormous house with its expensively furnished reception rooms, she caught a glimpse of the mother (always on the way to somewhere else), she suffered with the girl in the desolate nursery with its pale-green walls, its tidy doll's cupboard and its silence – and not only did her sympathy grow but also her desire to do everything in her power to comfort this clumsy, awkward and so shamefully neglected child; with every day that passed, increasingly and with ever greater conviction she began to consider this comforting as her duty, something that had been assigned to her and something she was firmly determined to carry out as well and as conscientiously as possible.

In this way the lessons with little Margaretha came to fill her whole existence. She planned them with the greatest of care, she looked forward to them, and whilst they lasted she felt happy – happy in a way she couldn't really fathom. She really loved these lessons. Indeed she loved the little girl's presence, her child-like trustfulness and her chatter. Sometimes, however, what the girl said made her uncertain, she felt increasingly uneasy the more detailed the little girl became and the more she elaborated on all the thousands of small cares which filled her working day. What have I myself got to recount? she then thought and the thought caused a slight giddiness. What can I really remember about the first nine years of my life? About my mother's and my life in Budapest? About the house, the street and yard where presumably I used to play?

"Mummy's promised we'll go to Wurstelprater Pleasure Gardens on Saturday," whispered Margaretha, in the middle of playing one Monday some time in March.

"This Saturday," she repeated with a laugh.

A short and slightly embarrassed laugh.

She and her mother, she explained, would first of all have a turn on the Big Wheel, the *Riesenrad,* to find out if you could see as far as their house in Gersthof from there. And then they would ride on the train through the whole park, eat frankfurters and buy lottery tickets, or at least one.

But best of all, she said, looking with a dreamy expression at the black and white keys in front of her, best of all they were going to have a ride on the merry-go-round.

"The same merry-go-round", she smiled, "as my mummy once rode when she was a girl".

"Dear child," Magda interrupted and laid her arm on her shoulder, "you haven't finished playing your piece yet."

*

104

Suddenly and with violent force she was hurled out of sleep, out of her bright, light, indeed almost transluscent morning sleep up towards the surface of wakefulness. An utterance (in her dream) had awakened her. A few disconnected words of which nothing now remained except a sharp echo, almost as clear as glass, an aural image without either meaning or cohesion.

The whole morning she was occupied with a single thought: what words had she really heard – with such strange clarity – and why had they in a fraction of a second made her wide awake? She puzzled over these words when having breakfast, when making the bed, cleaning and food-shopping at Gersthof, just as she puzzled over them in the afternoon when sitting at the piano and later in the evening when Thomas had come home a long time ago. Not even during their short and half-unreal love-making would the thoughts of these words give her any peace, it was really as if she carried the search for the words with her into her sleep and as if that in turn made her dreams even more elusive and anguished than they had been so far – she awoke next morning with a feeling of loss that was almost unbearable.

And now she seemed to remember that not only one voice but several were involved.

As if these voices had actually already been there earlier, in fact for a long time: the utterances and fragments of conversations which were still echoing so clearly within her but which could no longer be discerned as anything but sound. And of course it was just these incomprehensibe utterances that stood in the way of her dreams, yes, naturally it was all these transparent but also darkly significant voices that had prevented her for so long from bringing the dreams with her out of the darkness up into the light – the dreams and all the memories that lay concealed within them.

What's more, she soon realized something else, the voices seemed to emanate from her immediate surroundings – even if

they couldn't be interpreted she knew that they had no connec-
tion at all with her own native tongue, no, that they were all,
without exception, statements in this new, despite everything,
foreign language in which she was now forced to live.

This last thought filled her not only with horror but also with
the deepest despair.

And so, as a consequence of this and when another day or so
had elapsed, a strange insecurity began to exist within her.
What, she now had to ask herself, what was to be her position in
all this which, it was obvious, was going on incessantly around
her.

What shall I say when I meet the caretaker? she thought.

The local wives? Or the friendly tailor on the ground floor?

The strange thing was, it also occurred to her, that – in this
regard too – objects themselves played a role.

Indeed it was, she thought, as yet more time had elapsed, it
was as if the voices were to be found hidden in objects, as if all
the fragmentary utterances and exchanges of opinion that
whirled round in her mind emanated from them, from their very
surroundings – as if the voices survived just by transforming
themselves into scents and lights, into colours, shapes and
external perceptions.

She watched the snow falling outside the kitchen window
and had to ask herself immediately what the caretaker really
meant with all his talk about lotteries and illusory wins worth
millions, she passed the telephone and remembered her sister-
in-law's dark insinuations, she made the bed and heard
Thomas's laugh. And every time she smelled the scent of per-
fume, saw a flame fluttering or passed the florist's in Währinger
Strasse, she was immediately transported to the drawing-room
in Canovagasse. At such moments she imagined herself immediately enveloped in the pale-green light from the silk lamp-
shades, she thought she could taste the dinner they had just
finished (chilled artichoke soup or cheese-filled pasties, salmon

or slightly salted beef with horseradish), she heard someone strumming the baby grand piano, she saw that Elisabeth's blue silk rosette was as usual threatening to slip off at any moment, that little Erich was paler than ever and that Thomas constantly observed his father, indeed that with keen attention and strangely gleaming eyes he was following his father's slightest movement.

And out of all that, created out of a few words that had lain concealed in a smell or the glimpse of a bouquet of white roses, new and increasingly insistent voices emerged.

These days she would occasionally stay at home instead of going out.

She didn't really want to meet the caretaker.

No, she didn't want to meet the caretaker or the local wives, neither the tailor nor the shop assistant at the tobacconist's. She began to dread the thought that little Margaretha's mother would take it into her head to accompany her daughter to her piano lesson. And most of all she dreaded Saturday's lunch at Canovagasse: why, it suddenly struck her, why does nobody mention a single word about Hungary any more?

In fact why do they act in Thomas's family as if Hungary had ceased to exist?

Little Margaretha sat hunched on the piano stool. She was sitting directly in the pale sun from the balcony window, her chubby little fingers rested on the keys, her spectacles glistened.

"The swan," she whispered, "I think I'll choose the swan".

She had just shared with Magda at length and in detail her reflections on the visit the next day to Wurstelprater. As soon as she had arrived, in fact while still standing there on the doorstep holding her brown paper bag in front of her, half blinded and frostbitten, she had in triumphant tones declared that it was Friday today, and thus Saturday tomorrow, and there were barely twenty-four hours left before she and her mummy would go off to the pleasure gardens, barely twenty-four hours before they would do everything she had dreamt about for almost two weeks.

Before they would have a turn on the *Riesenrad*, take the train, eat frankfurters, buy lottery tickets – and best of all, ride on the merry-go-round.

"The swan," she whispered again, "or perhaps the white horse with a golden mane".

Then she looked at Magda and told her, for the third time that afternoon, about the photograph.

"It's slightly brownish," she said, "but perfectly distinct. Mummy's seven years old, she's wearing a black coat and a hat that's as white as the swan, her head is bent backwards and she's laughing loudly."

"Mummy," she said and gave the same introverted smile as before, "Mummy says she can't remember ever being so happy in her whole life as that time".

On Saturday the sun shone from a clear blue sky, the snow dripped from the roofs, the pigeons cooed. Magda suggested to Thomas that they should ring and cancel lunch at Canovagasse and take the bus instead up to Leopoldsberg and walk from there down to Nussdorf, she longed to get out, she said, and it was so long since they had done anything together. "It can't be done," Thomas said decisively, "we can't change our minds now".

He added with a shrug of his shoulders in a gesture at once apologetic and a touch disdainful, "We quite simply don't behave like that in my family".

On the way out he began to talk about his work at the clinic again. It had turned out, he said, that the little boy who had had a cold ever since birth lacked immune defences and had now started to be plagued by recurring fungus infections, white blisters which from the mouth and throat slowly spread over his

face. "You can be glad you don't have to see him," he added just
as they got off the tram at Schottentor, "it's not a pretty sight".
The clock in Votivkirche struck two. They hurried past the
university, City Hall and Parliament. In the corner of Baben-
bergerstrasse a car braked suddenly to allow three nuns to cross,
their black veils fluttering like magpies' wings in the light
breeze. Thomas watched them go, "I've always longed to see
them fly," he said thoughtfully, "perhaps because in some way
I've always connected them with my mother". Ten minutes later
they had reached Canovagasse. They approached in silence.
The maid in black helped them off with their coats. There was
a bouquet of white roses on the table in the hall. When the
sound of laughter penetrated from the drawing-room Magda's
brow suddenly broke out into a cold sweat and she was overwhelmed by an almost irresistible urge to turn and flee – instead
she took Thomas's outstretched arm and allowed herself with a
wildly beating heart, to be led into the drawing-room.

Only after a long while did she calm down slightly. Indeed, it
wasn't until the ceremonial greetings were over, she had drunk
two glasses of sekt and they had all sat down at the laid table in
the dining-room that her hands stopped shaking and she could
breathe normally. So much whiteness! she then thought, and
looked around her in dismay. How unnaturally white everything
is! Not only the table cloth and the roses, not only the aunt's
blouse, all the starched shirt fronts and the thin lace curtains,
but also little Erich's round face above the table edge – and for
that matter Uncle Karl's face just next to his. Yes, they are all so
strangely pale white, as if their foreheads and noses, cheeks,
chins and ears were made of porcelain.

And the conversation!

Naturally they had talked about von Karajan right from the
start. Indeed from the very first glass of sekt they had discussed
von Karajan's plans to produce *La Bohème* in the autumn; when
they had sat down at the table they had in increasingly loud

voices argued about the possible reasons for von Karajan having selected Leontyne Price as Leonora. Now the conversation seemed to have touched on several different things, of which she could distinguish only a fraction.

"Brilliant!"

"But nobody knows what really happened."

"It was about the worst…"

"…a little too fast, at least certain passages in Act Three…"

"In any case there'll still be trouble."

"Such a beautiful tone…"

"Icy! His music's about as beautiful as a sunlit Alpine landscape."

"…with an intensity and depth without equal."

But, she thought, why all these knowing smiles and short, significant laughs?

These strange pauses?

"I suppose the question is…" that was the aunt's voice.

"You've got the whole thing wrong!" cried Thomas's father.

"Austrian youth…" interrupted Uncle Karl, and then he broke off, looked thoughtfully at the white roses on the table, smiled and raised his glass.

"A toast to von Karajan," he said with a laugh. At that moment the doors were thrown open and the main course was carried in. They served themselves in silence. The girl in black disappeared out into the kitchen.

They started to eat. But what had that Moosbrugger really to do with von Karajan? "Stabbed twenty-five times" – this was the aunt again – "the poor girl was not only raped and strangled, she was positively slaughtered". "And inside the actual Opera House," Elise sighed, lowered her voice so that the children wouldn't hear and began a whispered conversation with the aunt. "Dagmar Fuhrich," Martin hissed to Thomas across the table, "A twelve-year-old at the ballet school. It happened the day before yesterday and now they're talking about nothing else over there."

Then suddenly there was silence again around the table. "My dear little friend," the aunt said absentmindedly, for the first time during lunch turning her attention towards Magda. "How's your piano pupil doing? Is she making any progress?"

"You know," she said to her brother in the same breath, "she's the one related to my friend Ginzkey, the children's writer, in fact his family comes from Fiume…"

"Penza, my dear.." interrupted Uncle Karl.

His sister shrugged and suggested that they should move. Outside, it had started to grow dark. The clock in Karlskirche struck four.

On only one single occasion had Magda asked Thomas about his mother's death, about the reason why she had died so young, before she had reached thirty-nine – his mother, she knew, had not been ill and her sudden death had obviously come as a shock to all the family. She remembered the occasion very well, in actual fact she would never forget how Thomas, in a fraction of a second, had changed from the friendliest frame of mind to something resembling rage suppressed with only the greatest difficulty. They had been sitting in a railway compartment, she could no longer remember whether it was three or four years ago, nor where they were actually bound for, the only thing she remembered was that they were alone in the compartment, that the snow was whirling past outside the windows and that Thomas, while dreamily observing the white landscape outside described his childhood summers in Burgenland. He described how his mother used to take the boys with her on long walks in the mountains and how when he was six years old and ill with scarlet fever she had spent hours playing with the puppet theatre for him and finally, when not even the wildest exploits on his bedside table which served as the stage made him laugh, she had burst into tears and promised him a puppy as soon as he was well again. "My mother promised me this against her better judgement," he had said, "because Father had always deplored the very thought of house pets". She had wanted to ask him if his mother had kept her promise (she couldn't remember Thomas ever having mentioned that he had had a dog as a child), instead for some reason she had blurted out the question about his mother's death – and with dismay had seen him give a start, grow pale and with tightly compressed lips declare that that was something he neither wished nor could talk about and that he forbade her to broach the subject ever again.

When on the morning after the lunch at Canovagasse she was woken, as so often lately, by the sound of the church bells penetrating her sleep the first conscious thought she had, despite Thomas's strictures, was that she would ask him again about his mother's death. Perhaps, she thought, while with a strange feeling of disorientation she heard the sound of the bells fade away, perhaps it was just the tolling of the bells that had given rise to this thought within her: Thomas's mother according to him had been a fervent Catholic, had attended Mass every Sunday, confessed regularly and always conscientiously said her prayers. The tolling of the bells or perhaps something else, something to do with yesterday's lunch but which she had already forgotten.

Thomas was asleep. It was still dark outside, in the faint light from the streetlamp it looked as though he was smiling in his sleep. He looks so peaceful, she thought, almost happy – and she decided not to say anything all the same. After an hour or so she got up and made some tea, then she woke him up.

They drank their tea in silence. Thomas had some ham and cheese on dark bread, she herself didn't want anything. After breakfast he asked if she would like to walk to the hospital with him, there were a few things, he said, that he had to check in the Department. She shook her head, muttered something about feeling chilly and in fact having a slight headache. When she saw his expression she hastened to assure him that it was nothing to worry about. She simply needed to rest a little and when he came back she would like to play the piano for him. Or perhaps they could have a game of chess, they hadn't played for a long time and she longed to take the revenge he had promised. He laughed, kissed her and set off.

She hadn't really wanted to be on her own but the thought of the clinic had frightened her somewhat, and now when she saw Thomas disappear across the courtyard she was seized with a strange unease. Suddenly she didn't know how to make the time pass until he returned. She ought to wash up the breakfast dishes, but all at once she felt too tired for that. She couldn't make herself wash up, read or even sit down at the piano. Instead she walked restlessly back and forth over the carpet in the living room. At some time she stopped and looked at the telephone. I ought to ring somebody, she thought. But then she couldn't think whom she should ring in that case, no, when she realized that there really wasn't a single person she wanted to talk to, she put the matter out of her head and continued instead her increasingly anguished wandering back and forth over the dark-red carpet. I wonder if Thomas's mother used to read aloud to him, she thought, to him and to his brothers – and at the same time realized that she had been standing staring as if hypnotized at something that looked like a flower, perhaps a lily, in the carpet's twining leaf-pattern. Then she pulled herself together, hurried to get yesterday's newpaper and snuggled into the sofa.

The paper was filled with news about the poor ballet girl Dagmar Fuhrich. Earlier, at breakfast, she had accorded the various articles only a distracted interest, the headlines had repelled her, as had the recollection of the whispered conversation Elise had had with her aunt at lunch the previous day; now reluctantly she became absorbed in them. With mounting horror she went into all the details surrounding the brutal murder, she read about all twenty-five stab wounds, about how the lacerated body had been found in the ballet dancers' shower-room on the second floor and about the traces of blood on the stairs to the third floor. Dagmar Fuhrich was an unusually pretty girl, she learnt, but also unusually shy; she had complained in disgust that only a fortnight before the murder a strange young man had taken her by the waist and lifted her into the air. Her father, the paper said, had been indignant at her story and had urged his daughter never to allow anything like that to happen again and to shout for help immediately if a strange man so much as came near her. But on the occasion of the murder she had not shouted. Had she recognized the murderer? Was the perpetrator somebody connected with the building? Another thing pointed to that. Presumably the murderer had waited for the girl hidden behind a curtain, in a cubbyhole outside the shower room which usually served as a changing room for the members of the chorus. But how could an outsider know about this place? And what business could the girl have had anyway on the second floor when the ballet school premises were on the fourth? At 4.15 p.m. she read, the girl had left home in Boltzmanngasse, at 4.45 p.m. she had arrived at the Opera. The murder had been committed at most only a few minutes later and after approximately a further ten minutes had been discovered. The police, nevertheless, had not been called to the spot until 5.35 p.m., that is to say more than half-an-hour after the discovery. Why?

Magda shivered.

There was a photograph of the girl too. After having read through all the articles carefully she went on to examine in detail the picture of the tender, smiling twelve-year-old in a white dress, black leggings and ballet shoes. She noticed that the girl had assumed a slightly coquettish pose rather reminiscent of that of a mature woman, that she had small white flowers in her hair and that her head was held slightly to the side. She pored over the picture and tried to conjure up the living person behind it, tried to imagine the girl waking up in her bed in the flat in Boltzmanngasse, dressing and drawing her hair-brush through her thick dark hair, saying goodbye to her dog, dashing down the stairs, curtseying to the neighbours and finally, at her mother's side, waiting for the tram to take her to the Opera House – to the Opera House and to the terrible death which now, for the observer, bestowed on the picture of her small form a special luminosity, an intense and almost magical radiance.

Magda couldn't take her eyes off the picture – for some strange reason it made her think again about Thomas's mother. And after a while she noticed to her horror that the longer she looked at the picture of the murdered ballet pupil the more the picture of Thomas's mother intervened, so that in the end one picture was no longer distinguishable from the other, so that in fact the two pictures had really fused into one. And at the same time it occurred to her that both these beings, who had thus become one, existed exclusively in her own imagination, that admittedly they moved, laughed and threw their soft white arms in a caressing gesture round their mother's neck or their children's shoulders, as if on a brightly lit stage, but that this stage existed only in her mind's eye – and it suddenly struck her that the dead ballet pupil as well as Thomas's dead mother in some obscure way was connected with her own life. Yes, all at once she felt convinced that all this talk about Moosbrugger, about criminals and victims, about mental aberration, guilt and man's innate evil with all its insinuations, ooh-ing and aah-ing and exclamations of horror, were really intended as a message aimed at just her. And hardly had she thought this thought through when she happened to think about another thing, something which at first glance could seem irrelevant but which all the same she felt intuitively was connected: she remembered how they laughed at her in the greengrocer's.

For surely it was her they were laughing at?

She had just asked if the shop had got any oranges in –

according to the *Neuer Kurier* blood oranges from Seville should have been available in the town for about a week – when everybody in the shop, not only the greengrocer but all the other customers too, began to laugh. Presumably, she now thought, they weren't laughing at what she had said but the way she had said it. For she knew of course that even if by now she had mastered the foreign language very well, both the grammar and the vocabulary, there was always something in the actual accent that betrayed her, some slight deviation in the intonation – always, she thought, some nook or cranny into which they could smuggle their inquisitive glances and their thick, prying fingers.

When at that moment the telephone rang she couldn't bring herself to answer it. Let it ring, she thought. And then, without properly knowing what she meant by it: they have only themselves to blame.

When Thomas came home an hour or so later she said: "Your aunt was laughing at me yesterday, she was laughing at the way I speak."

Thomas looked at her unsympathetically. "Have you gone mad?" he said. "That's one of the most ludicrous things I've ever heard."

"What was your aunt laughing at, then?" she insisted. "Just as we were about to leave, when she asked where I'd found my dress and I answered that you'd bought it for my birthday."

Thomas smiled slightly.

"Ah," he said in a vague voice, "that – well, it's rather difficult to explain to someone who doesn't directly belong to the family."

On Monday little Margaretha came a few minutes late. She stood there inside the doorway, timid and irresolute. She didn't smile and she didn't hold out the brown paperbag in front of her. Magda hurried to close the door behind her, help her off with her coat, hat, mittens and her small galoshes and guide her into the living-room. She led her to the piano and placed her on the piano stool. There she stood for a long while observing the little girl in silence. The little girl sat huddled, looking down at her lap. Magda hesitated. She suspected what had happened and her suspicions wakened the strangest and most contradictory emotions within her. Pity, yes, above all pity. But something else too. Something that most of all resembled distaste, a profound and terrible distaste, the cause of which she couldn't understand.

But which made her ashamed. In some undefined way feel guilty.

And this in turn, she noticed immediately to her horror, made her furious.

She took a deep breath. Then she forced herself to sit beside the girl on the piano stool, she also managed to make herself, as tender-hearted as before, place her arm on her shoulders.

"Well?" she asked in a low voice, "how was it? Did you choose the swan? Or the horse with the golden mane after all?"

Little Margaretha snuffled. She hunched down even further and barely noticeably shook her head.

Of course, Magda thought. What else could you expect.

Aloud she said: "Tell me! Now let me hear about it!"

And Margaretha mumbled something about it having been too cold. About the wind and the unusual cold. "Although", she then said and cleared her throat, "Mummy did promise...

" ...and once it gets warmer..."

Then she looked up at Magda: "Mummy has promised," she said and now she smiled cautiously, "Mummy has promised that we'll go as soon as it's spring".

Magda made no reply. Instead she asked Margaretha to take out her book and play her piece. The remainder of the lesson passed without their mentioning a word about Saturday's cancelled visit to Wurstelprater. Margaretha couldn't play her little piece and Magda insisted that they wouldn't finish until she had got through it passibly at least once. When the clock struck three she had got halfway and Magda urged the girl to learn the piece properly for next time. Just as Margaretha was about to get up from the piano stool she unexpectedly held Magda back.

"Have...? she murmured. "Have...?"

Magda observed her carefully.

"Yes?" she said. "What is it you want to know?"

Margaretha looked down. Then she asked in a whispering voice if she, Magda, at some time when she was little, had visited an amusement park with her mother, not with her grandmother but with her real mother, her from Budapest.

Magda froze. Good heavens, she thought, why's she asking that? She knows very well how difficult it is for me to remember the slightest event from my childhood, indeed how many times have I explained to her that I've hardly any mental pictures at all from my time in Budapest, that it was so long ago and that so much has come in between. Oh, she thought bitterly, she knows what I'll answer. That's why she's asking, to hear me say that I never had an outing like that with my mother either.

Which, of course, I haven't, she thought.

She didn't know whether to laugh or cry.

There was a short pause, then she suddenly bent forward, took the girl by the chin and forced her to look her in the eyes.

"Oh yes!" she heard herself say. "Of course I went to an amusement park with my mother. And not just once but many times, in fact so many times I've lost count."

And then without being able to stop herself she described to Margaretha all the Sundays in her childhood on which her mother had taken her with her to the amusement park on the Buda side. She explained that she and her mother had lived in Pest, in the street in Józsefvaros that borders the river and that from their large room they had had the most fantastic view over Buda and the amusement park, in fact when the traffic calmed

down towards evening they had been able to hear all the shrieks
and laughter from there. The park was so close to their house
that they could walk there, she said, and although really feeling
slightly ashamed she couldn't help going on to give in detail an
account of the packed lunch her mother used to prepare (juice,
meat pasties and cakes with walnut cream filling, just the sort
her mother knew that she, Magda, was particularly fond of) or
continuing her story maintaining that despite their packed
lunch they used to buy ice-cream from the stall inside the gates,
that her mother used to stand leaning over the fence around the
merry-go-round and look out for her when she was having a
ride, that they waved to each other and laughed every time it
went round and that her mother, even if she happened to be
tired, was the most beautiful mother in the whole amusement
park.

Here she broke off. She was no longer looking at the girl in
front of her. With unseeing eyes she observed instead the black
house tops on the other side of the courtyard – suddenly terrified at the abyss of darkness that had opened within her.

"My mother", she concluded in a helpless whisper, "always
used to wear a blue shawl, a light-blue shawl that was the same
colour as the sky above her head".

She gave a start, discovered that she was still holding little
Margaretha by the chin and released her in dismay. Then she
quickly explained that it was already past three o'clock and that
it was high time for the girl to leave.

That same night, as well as her usual diffuse and fleeting dream
fragments Magda dreamed something that took the form of a
sequence of events, a nightmare which also lingered in her consciousness after she had woken up.

In the dream, for the first time since her escape, she was back
in Sopron. She had got there by bus – and not alone but in the
company of József.

But József had vanished.

She ran around in Sopron looking for him, she searched everywhere, and while she was hurrying up and down the streets, while looking through cellars, deserted houses and strange, dark passages, it suddenly dawned on her that József hadn't really vanished when they had got off the bus at all, but that he had already been missing for several days, perhaps in fact for several weeks.

Her anxiety in the dream intensified.

Then she found herself in a street somewhere near a green-grocer's in Lenin Körút. A van was parked by the pavement and it was just as she was passing it, just as she was on the point of hurrying past it, that she discovered József – the boy was lying motionless under the driver's seat, his body was pale, limp and slightly swollen and the look he directed towards her was filled with despair.

She cried out – but without a sound passing her lips.

She rushed forward to the van. She pulled József out of the driver's cab and pressed him tightly to her. But – in vain. Having finally found him was to no avail – no matter how she shook him, how she kissed him, cradled him and appealed to him to wake up, he remained just as limp, lifeless and silently accusing the whole time. At the very moment that she realized that he was dead she was hurled with violent force up towards the surface of consciousness.

She was bathed in sweat, her heart was pounding. For a short while she considered whether she should wake Thomas up and tell him about her dream, then she rejected the thought, no, telling Thomas about it was pointless, she knew in advance what would happen. Admittedly he would do everything to calm her, but her dream would also make him afraid and in his fear he would start to argue, emphasize, as he always had done at the beginning of their acquaintanceship, that József was not really her child, that she had had no right to keep him and that she must free herself from her past once and for all. You must finally learn to forget, he would say.

After that he would kiss her – and, admittedly against her will, she would succumb to his caresses.

No, in no circumstances would she wake up Thomas. Instead she got up, sneaked out of the bedroom on tiptoe and sat down at the table in the dark kitchen. Her thoughts whirled around within her, she felt frightened by the dream, horrified at what it had revealed to her – the terrible guilt to which she had tried to close her eyes for so long. Oh, she thought, I have acted so wrongly! I did so wrong when I listened to the others, to the refugee camp doctor, the Red Cross staff and later to Thomas too, it was so wrong of me to believe their assurances, their kindly but false assurances that not only must I forget the past but that I must also give the boy the opportunity to begin his new life without heart-rending memories.

His new life! she said to herself repeatedly. His new life! And while she remained sitting there at the kitchen table shivering with cold, while instead of going back to bed and lying down again and trying to go back to sleep she saw night slowly turning into dawn, she could feel how a decision slowly and inexorably was forming within her. When morning came she also knew what she had to do – that very day she would seek out the letter that she had received five years ago from József's foster mother, she would seek out the letter, defy the others and finally write to the boy.

2

She searched for a long time. At last she found the letter right at the back of one of the drawers in Thomas's writing desk. She couldn't understand how it had landed up there, whether she herself had put it there or whether Thomas had found it and decided to hide it away. Or whether on that occasion so long ago she had given it to him to read – read and perhaps give her some advice. But one thing she was sure of: if he really had given her advice it would have been to forget, to put the letter away and stop thinking about it.

And of course that was what had happened.

Now she took the letter with her out into the kitchen, it was lighter there. She sat down at the table, swept a few non-existent crumbs off the wax table cloth and laid the letter down in front of her without being able to bring herself to see what it contained: her heart was beating so strongly and heavily in her breast that she wanted to wait a little. It was only after fetching a glass of tea from the teapot on the bench, only after she had drunk small sips of the tepid liquid for a long time, followed the neighbourhood boys' game of football in the sunlit courtyard below, that she plucked up courage, took out the letter, opened it out and began to read. It was a brief letter. An account of how the boy had been met at the ferry in Trelleborg, of the train journey between Trelleborg and Malmö, of the new home in the outskirts of the town and the room that the boy had all to himself, of the foster parents' hope that the boy would get on well, of how very fond he seemed to be of sweets, his touching small fits of anger which they hoped they would soon be able to get him out of and his silence. He is so silent, it said, that one could almost believe that he has already forgotten all his Hungarian.

She read the last sentence again and again. And now? she thought. How much can he remember now, after almost six years?

There was also a photograph in the envelope. She couldn't remember having seen it before. It was a black-and-white photo, obviously taken by an amateur or by someone who had been in a great hurry: the picture was not only blurred, it had been taken slightly at an angle so that the little boy and the adults on each side of him were leaning dangerously over to the right. The boy in the picture was staring earnestly straight at the observer. The light that came in obliquely from behind made his ears look like a bat's, added to which the light elongated the adults' shadows to an enormous length – something which strengthened the impression that the three characters with or against their will would at the next moment fall forward at an angle and so disappear without trace out of the picture.

She looked at the small figure in the centre of the picture for a long time. What was he brooding about? she asked herself. Why is he keeping his hands stuck down so deeply in the pockets of his short coat? And what does he think of the smiling woman in a hat on his right side and the bare-headed man on his left, the man who is holding a briefcase in one hand and who is holding his shoulder in such a heavy grip with the other – what does he think of these foreign people of whose language he still doesn't understand a word?

What shall I ask him about? she thought. What shall I tell him myself?

In fact to whom shall I actually write my letter?

At that moment she felt that Thomas was standing behind her. She hadn't heard him unlock the outer door. Surprised, she gave a start and hurriedly laid her hand over the letter. "Thomas…" she said, "I never heard you come in" – but when she turned around with a smile, there was nobody there.

The letter was soon to prove more difficult to write than she could have imagined. It took her almost a week to find even a way of starting it. Who, again and again she had to ask herself, who is it really that I am writing to? József is ten years old now, and although he's quite probably small for his age – but he must be so incredibly bigger than when I last saw him. Now she sat at the kitchen table as she had done every morning that week; in just a few hours little Margaretha would be coming. Today too the sun was shining, today too the boys from next door were playing football down in the courtyard, she could hear their light voices all the way up here.

It occurred to her all at once that presumably József too liked to kick a ball. That he no doubt spent a great deal of his spare time playing football: dashing excitedly back and forth somewhere in a yard that perhaps in many ways resembled this one. It also suddenly struck her, perhaps he can play the piano. Yes, she decided at that moment, József is short for his age, he's slim but not actually thin and nowadays he has quite long hair which curls slightly at the sides. He prefers to play defence rather than attack, he has many friends at school, he does his homework most dutifully in the evenings and he surprises everybody around him by at only ten years of age being an extraordinarily proficient pianist. And as for having forgotten all his Hungarian, she thought, that's only something he pretends. Something he simulates in order to safeguard his innermost and most precious secrets. Yes, she thought, that's just it! And it occurred to her just then that that too was something they had in common, she and József, something that united them, something, she thought, that had existed between them during all the six years that had passed since the abrupt and unreal parting in Traiskirchen – even if she had been unaware of it until now. And that, she continued, was a further reason why she must write to him, in fact, she told herself, for that very reason it was her duty that she got in touch with him – in Hungarian.

In the language that was theirs!

In the language that was concealed in their heart, she realized now, that permeated their very being. It was also this thought, the thought of everything that bound them together, that finally caused her to pick up her pen and start to write. "Dear József," she wrote (and she couldn't help smiling at the thought of how on that occasion he had acquired his name), "Dear József, you're already ten years old and play both football and the piano. It will soon be six years since we parted. Now please don't think…" Oh, she thought and stopped, why am I writing like that? Why should he think that I've forgotten him? That I've simply ignored him all these years? That I've not been in touch because of lack of interest or pure laziness? No, she thought, naturally he won't believe anything like that – and soon realized, with a thrill of anticipation, that this conviction of hers was founded in the actual language. In the sudden meeting with her native tongue, with these words from which she had been separated for so long, these wonderful sound images that now overwhelmed her with their power, their light and their unexpected scent. She was affected by a slight trembling, suddenly felt euphoric and almost faint with relief. Naturally, she thought, naturally he's known all the time that I would write to him as soon as the time was right.

She cast a fleeting glance out of the window: the boys, she observed, had now gone over to roller-skating and in the gardens behind the white statue a cat was moving stealthily. She bit her pen, hesitated, then bent again over the paper and crossed out the last words. Instead she wrote: "You must

126

know…", hesitated again, considered and then completed the sentence: "…that during all these years I have never ceased to think about you." Then she let the pen sink down and again looked out over the courtyard. The sun was high in the sky, the pigeons were waddling heavily over the gleaming tin roof, and the plane trees, she noticed to her surprise, seemed almost about to turn green. It's true, she thought happily, even if I haven't realized it, József has always been there in my thoughts. She sank into a reverie. She smiled sometimes to herself. When the clock in St Leopoldskirche struck two she started in horror – and it then took her several seconds to become aware again of where she was.

This time little Margaretha behaved exactly as usual. She had hardly crossed the threshold before holding out the brown paper bag in front of her, she smiled all over her face, and as soon as Magda had placed her on the stool in front of the piano, in fact before she had even made an attempt to start playing her piece, she explained that her mummy had now also promised that she would be able to take one of her classmates with her to Wurstelprater and that it was definite that they were going, if not tomorrow when her mummy was otherwise engaged, then in a week or two at the very most.

Little Margaretha gave a laugh. Then she placed her little round hands on the keys and began to play. Now she really did know her piece. She must have practised properly, for not only could she play the whole of the little melody right to the end, she played it really well. She then gave a sigh of relief, raised her head and fixed her short-sighted expectant gaze on Magda's lips.

Against her will Magda gave a shudder.

Suddenly it was as if everything about the girl made her uneasy – as if everything about the small child gave rise to the greatest feeling of discomfort or quite simply contempt: not

just the girl's clumsy figure, her shyness and the pathetic vulnerability which so far had appealed so strongly to her pity, but
also, and not least, the childlike confidence with which she was
now awaiting an answer. How repulsive she is, she thought hor-
ror-stricken, and how shapelessly pale and swollen her small
hands rest there in her lap.

She knew that she ought to say something friendly, that she
ought to praise the girl's performance and that she ought to get
up immediately and fetch the stars (she had actually forgotten
to stick one in last time). Yet she couldn't make herself do either
one or the other. Instead she murmured something inaudible,
something which at a pinch could be interpreted as a kindness,
then she stroked the girl's hair fleetingly and explained that the
piece they were now to play was considerably more difficult
than the previous one, that both persistence and skill were
required to learn it, but that she nevertheless expected that
Margaretha would be able to play straight through it next time.

Little Margaretha nodded. She no longer smiled, but it was
impossible to decide whether her earnestness was the result of
disappointment or if she was proud of the assignment she had
just been given. Then Magda was ashamed. And when the lesson was over and she had gone to the door with Margaretha she
forced herself, even if with the greatest distaste, to bend down
and on parting give the little girl a kiss on the cheek.

That same evening she told Thomas about the letter: about
her decision to write to József, despite the fact that so much time
had elapsed, nevertheless to get in touch with him. She felt, she
said, that she must do so – as much for her own sake as for his.

Thomas had just stretched out his hand for the matches on
the occasional table. Now he stopped in the middle of the movement and looked at her blankly.

"I now also know", Magda continued, "that József still
understands Hungarian and that he has only been waiting all
these years for a sign from my side".

At these words Thomas ground his cigarette to pieces.
"Magda!" he almost yelled.

"Dear Magda," he appealed in a voice that had soon sunk to
a whisper. And when at that moment she met his gaze she saw
that he was not only upset – he was afraid, or rather: horrified.

The sun was shining, spring was in the air and down in Aumannplatz the broom was in flower. She got off the tram in Spitalgasse, crossed over Währinger Strasse and turned to the left
into Strudlhofgasse. She walked slowly. Let herself be suffused
with light, warmth and the slightly acid smell of sun-warmed
brick. Here in the smaller streets it was also quiet and peaceful.
A feeling of elation had come over her, of anticipation, and she
smiled to herself at the thought of how a while ago she had nodded to the caretaker when she had met him in the courtyard, in
fact how she had even said something about the weather, about
how it would in any case be some time before he would need to
worry about shovelling snow again. He looked surprised, she
thought contentedly and crossed a street she didn't know the
name of, he no doubt went there agonizing about the next lottery draw. In the little square above the steps down towards Pas-
teurgasse two young lads were kicking a ball, on the bench
under the small tree, right next to the wall, an old woman was
sitting knitting. Magda nodded benignly to her when she went
past. I shall ask József if he has a bicycle, she thought just as she
noticed the old woman raise her head from her knitting and
shout to one of the boys, I shall ask him if he usually cycles to
school or if he has so far to go that he has to take a tram or a bus.

Down by the fountain she stopped for a moment, took out a
coin and threw it into the water below the brown fish's stone
head. In any case, when he comes here, she thought, we shall
take the bus up Leopoldsberg, he'll be delighted at the view
from the monastery gardens. The number 38 bus, she murmured to herself absentmindedly, or maybe number 40; then

she looked around quickly but there was not a soul in sight, the marble steps shone white and the green railings gave the impression that it really was already summer.

In June, she decided at the moment she continued to walk down towards Liechtensteinstrasse, he must come here in June at the latest, preferably by the end of May. Yes, she thought, while giving way to an enormous light-blue pram, as soon as they open for the season József and I shall hire bicycles and cycle to Gänzehäufel and go bathing. Just as she was passing Liechtenstein Palace a dog began to bark in the grounds; a man's voice ordered it to be quiet. On the pavement a little girl was jumping with both feet into a puddle. She thought she ought to urge the girl to be careful, to point out to her that the warmth was deceptive at this time of year and that it was easy to catch a chill, but just as she was about to open her mouth to say a few kindly words the girl turned abruptly and disappeared into the palace yard. Slightly losing her composure she herself continued down towards the next street where, however, she was soon deep in thought again – she now thought about how happy József would be at the prospect of going by train all the way to Vienna, how he would boast to his friends about his forthcoming journey and how eagerly he would prepare everything in the tiniest detail. In the very next letter, she thought, I'll write to him about this and then I mustn't forget to ask him if possible to pack his football. His football, she thought and remained standing as though transfixed – only now did she discover, to her horror, that she was outside the school in Glasergasse.

What am I doing here? ran through her mind. How have I landed up here anyway, right in front of the school entrance and visible to anyone who happens to cast a glance out of the window?

She turned quickly and hurried away. She had reached Alserbachstrasse before calming down a little. I must be on my guard, she then thought (without really knowing what she meant by that).

From now on I must be much more cautious.

On arriving home she was seized with an inexplicable weariness. She lay down on the sofa to rest but fell immediately into a heavy, trance-like sleep. When she awoke Thomas had come home. He had bought a bag of black grapes on the way from the clinic, he maintained that they were stuffed with vitamins, put the grapes on the table in front of her and urged her to eat some while he made some tea. Whilst they were drinking it he told her that Martin had bought a new mandolin and that it seemed that an epidemic of infantile paralysis was about to break out in Budapest. She listened in silence, then she said that she wanted to read a poem for him.

In Hungarian.

From the only book that she had had enough presence of mind to take with her when she escaped.

She did so. She read slowly, as if weighing every word in her hand before proffering it to him, so that perhaps, despite the fact that he really understood nothing, he could nevertheless comprehend something of its deeper import – but also in an attempt to conceal her agitation.

"You were so different," Thomas said when she fell silent.

She gave a laugh.

"I used to read this poem to the girls at school," she said, "to my pupils in Sopron. Attila József wrote it in a single night at a café – it is a homage to Thomas Mann who was to visit Budapest the next day. The beginning is so wonderful, with the child's plea for a story as solace in the darkness.

"In Attila József's world," she said, "adults live as strangers in reality, shut up within themselves – it's only the children who're really alive.

"Attila József", she said, "loved children".

"Everything about you changed," Thomas continued as if he hadn't heard, "not only your voice but equally your face. Your eyes grew darker, your lips rounder, your cheeks had more colour – in fact one almost had the impression that your whole being grew a little, about a centimetre or two."

He said it in a peculiar, almost harsh tone and she had the feeling that the change he was talking about was not something he appreciated.

She looked at him thoughtfully.

"Perhaps I shall write to my grandparents too," she added after a while. "It could well be that the letters I once wrote so many years ago really did reach them. That in fact they did receive my letters – and that their reply quite simply got lost on the way."

That night, for the first time since her escape, or really since even much further back, she dreamt about her mother.

In the dream she saw her mother moving in a strongly lit room, alone, as if on a stage. She herself was outside the room, an observer in the dark, and it was just the fact that she couldn't bring herself to enter the course of events but remained an outside observer that was what the dream was really about. She saw her mother, noticed that the room where her mother was standing was a kitchen (perhaps even the kitchen in her childhood flat in Budapest), and from the first moment she was seized with an overwhelming joy, a feeling of happiness so strong that she wanted to cry out loud. She saw her mother turn her head towards her, saw the light that fell over her face, saw her laugh – and she saw finally how she opened her mouth to say something.

It was at that moment that the dream was transformed.

For of what her mother said, of the words that she herself in that first ecstatic moment thought were directed just at her, she could not register the slightest sound, and although in the despair that soon overpowered her she then shouted to her mother that she was there, despite her shouting desperately and trying in every way to attract her mother's attention, she soon realized that her mother had not noticed her, indeed at the moment she understood that her mother's words were silent it became obvious to her that her mother in actual fact couldn't see her – since her mother existed irrevocably in another time, in a room which was as separated from her own as the film screen's reality from the viewer.

She was awakened by her crying.

It was still dark outside. Thomas was asleep.

But this time she did wake him. She shook him roughly, raised herself up in the bed and, in a kind of desperate fury and whilst he, still half-asleep, groped for the cigarettes on the bedside table, she began to give an account of her dream. She described everything in detail. She described her mother's strongly illuminated, smiling face, her joy at first and the pain and sorrow which overwhelmed her as soon as she had realized that she herself was invisible and her mother impossible to reach. What had frightened her most, she declared, was the darkness, the darkness that surrounded the circle of light within which her mother moved, the darkness and her own impotence.

Thomas drew her towards him.

For a long while they lay silently, staring out into the semi-darkness in front of them. Why can I no longer remember my mother? passed through Magda's mind. Why are my memories so elusive and so vague? So shadow-like? Why do they disappear as soon as I turn my eyes towards them? I know that my mother used to take home proof-reading from the publishers and that she used to sit working in the kitchen far into the night, I know that she smoked a lot, that she detested the black, oily soot from the coal fire, that she suffered from having to leave me alone during the day, that she had a blue shawl and that she used to make chestnut purée and cakes with walnut filling for my birthday. But I have no memories of this. All this is something that could very well have been told me, details from somebody else's life, from a childhood that wasn't mine. My mother, she asked

133

herself again, our life together, and the places: the house we lived in, the courtyard where I must have spent such a large part of my childhood, the street and all the other dilapidated blocks there in Józsefvaros – why is all that as if expunged from my consciousness?

"Magda," whispered Thomas, "Magda, look at me!"

But she continued to stare obstinately into the darkness in front of her. A peculiar feeling had come over her when she heard his appeal, a blend of horror, tenderness and something that most of all resembled defiance.

Then she suddenly heard herself say (in a voice significantly steadier than before): "In the dream I was back in Budapest. In the house in Szigony utca in Józsefvaros where I lived together with my mother for the first nine years of my life."

She stopped at that.

Pushed her hair from her face, hesitated.

"I remember that a chestnut tree grew in the courtyard," she went on, while wondering to herself why she was lying to him, "a large tree that we children used to climb around in and whose shiny conkers we used to fill our pockets with in the autumn. I remember that the old men used to play chess under the tree and that there was always washing hanging up to dry.

"I remember too the smell of dustbins and gas," she said.

"And I remember particularly well that my mother used to sing when she ground walnuts in the rusty little grinder which was really intended for poppy seeds.

"My mother..." she said – but lost the thread.

She heaved a deep sigh. Then she twisted out of his embrace, sat up in the bed, threw her arms around her knees and looked at him: "One day," she said, "one day when circumstances are different I shall go back there. One day I shall return to the house in Szigony utca, find my way to the third floor and ask permission to see the small flat where I slept behind a screen in the same room as my mother."

She didn't mention with a single word on the other hand that she knew very well that not only their house but the whole of the neighbourhood had been obliterated in a bomb attack during the final phase of the war.

After she had been wholly taken up with thoughts of the letter for a further few days, after she had sat down at the kitchen table now and again to write a paragraph, to examine the words tentatively, reject them and instead again find new words for those already found (new and unexpected words which gave yet another dimension to what was already written), and after each time she set to work with the same wonderful feeling of solemnity and anticipation she suddenly noticed that some kind of change was on the way – the satisfaction which dealing with the letter afforded her slowly began to wane, indeed it occurred increasingly often that the almost intoxicating excitement that seized her when she held the pen slowly changed to the opposite: the light frame of mind gave way to an ever duller, darker feeling of disappointment.

It was fine as long as she addressed herself in the letter to József with questions and thoughts around his life: to discern ever more clearly the picture of his character made her happy, to feel how day after day he came ever closer to her always afforded her the same satisfaction, indeed to experience his presence so strongly that she could see him play among the other children in the yard out there, could hear his laughter or, on rare occasions, feel the slight touch of his arms round her neck, filled her not only with the most exultant joy but also with gratitude. The change came about when she had to tell József about herself: as soon as she came to the point in the letter where she proceeded to tell him how her life had taken shape since their parting in Traiskirchen she was seized with uncertainty, as soon as she tried to describe life here in Vienna it was as if she completely lost her way. A strange, almost paralysing inertia came over her – an inertia which, the longer she then forced herself to stick to her own story, slowly turned into disappointment. In this feeling of disappointment which every day grew stronger and more anguished, of emptiness and finally also: of fear. Indeed as soon as she made an attempt to write something about her life together with Thomas here in Hockegasse it was as if the words were void of meaning and significance. As if they soon lost their lustre. It was, she realized with mounting horror, as if everything around her was suddenly on the point of losing its import or, quite simply, as if the darkness into which her past had sunk, now, when she was trying to find words for all the new elements, was slowly overflowing its banks, as if in small rivulets it was penetrating her world in order to swallow up, one after another, the objects and phenomena of which her everyday life was constructed.

Suddenly she could no longer understand the point of the whole thing. What had all this that surrounded her to do with her? In what way was it connected just with her? The flat with its light, its shadows and its increasingly hollow silence, the courtyard where the caretaker seemed to rule absolutely, the streets, the parks or the never-ceasing stream of passing strangers? Thomas's family (who were of course just his and not hers) or Thomas himself?

Or for that matter, she thought, little Margaretha?

No, especially not little Margaretha. For the strange thing was, she had noticed it soon enough, that the longer she dealt with the letter, the clearer a picture of József emerged and the more she tried to find words for her own life, the more difficulty she seemed to have in abiding the girl's presence – the more she wrote the more repugnant and pitiful she found everything about the little girl, and especially then, as earlier, her vulnerability. Why, she asked herself, must the girl persist with her nonsense about Wurstelprater? And why must she look at me the whole time with those trusting and dog-like appealing eyes?

She was seized with despair. And how would she now ever be able to finish the letter? How could she finish it at all? She tried to force herself nevertheless to formulate something about herself, at least some hint of a description – József must of course, she said to herself, be told after all what was awaiting him here. But all her efforts were in vain: as soon as she put pen to paper the terrible inertia came over her and the pen slipped out of her hand as if of its own accord and fell back down on to the table.

Nevertheless she didn't want to give up.

And when after yet more time had elapsed without her having found a single meaningful formulation she decided to save all the details about herself for a later occasion. She wrote a final version of everything concerning József, rounded off the whole thing with a promise that soon, in fact in her very next letter, she would tell him more about herself, added an assurance of how much she loved him and finally, with some trepidation, wrote her name – before folding the letter, putting it in an envelope and printing József's name and address (which amazingly enough was included in the letter from Sweden) in large, clear letters on the front and her own address on the back. In order to be sure that the letter would be dispatched as soon as possible she went to the post office on Währinger Strasse with it. And a few minutes later, at the very moment she stepped out on to the street again, she had already started with feverish eagerness to await a reply.

She had a long wait. The days passed and became weeks.

The heat had now come in earnest, the evenings were long and light, the chestnuts were in bloom.

The first sign (she soon realized that it was indeed a sign) she discovered by chance: just as she alighted from the tram at Schottentor and at the very moment the Votivkirche clock struck three she noticed a balloon slowly disappearing in over the centre of the town.

She stood still, unsure on this first occasion of how to interpret what she had seen. The subsequent signs on the other
hand, at least seemed to her almost always at first glance to be
easier both to recognize and to understand. A few boys were
playing football in Aumannplatz and she knew straight away
that if any of them scored a goal before the tram had passed
(which fortunately did happen!) it meant that the letter from
József would arrive within the next few days. She caught a
glimpse of the caretaker's dark-clad figure over beside the dustbins and was soon afraid that he wouldn't speak to her (nevertheless she tried not to cheat by hanging back on the steps or
attracting his attention in any other way) – when he finally did
catch sight of her, when he hurried over to her and, in his usual
whispering, slightly insinuating voice asked if she had seen anything of the neighbours' boy's runaway cat her knees grew weak
with relief (even if the business with the cat wasn't really so
nice). And late one afternoon when she first heard the whirring
of the tailor's sewing machine stop just as she went through the
door and when soon after that she happened to meet two neighbours' wives and they both greeted her with a friendly smile she
hurried to the letter-box, convinced that the letter had arrived
while she was out. With her heart pounding with anticipation
she unlocked the small box (the one furthest to the right in the
top row) – only to find that it was empty as usual.

Otherwise Thomas was the most important.

It was, she soon realized, his habits, his topics of conversation
and the various information on times (something to which
strangely enough she hadn't given a thought before) that shaped
his existence, that completely decided whether her waiting
would be crowned with success. Some of his doings disturbed
her, in fact some of his utterances made her really uneasy – such
as the fact that he seemed to love to tell her about his aunt's (and
also his colleagues') speculations about the terrible murder of
little Dagmar Fuhrich (it wasn't difficult to see, of course, that

the speculations round the unknown murderer must be interpreted as bad omens). Nor did she like his habit of rolling his cigarette for a long while between thumb and index finger before lighting it or his questions about how the lessons were going, if that little Margaretha was making any progress and if she herself didn't consider it time to take on a few more pupils. Finally she also feared his sleep – the way that he not only seemed to sleep so deeply but also that his sleep seemed to be completely free from dreams.

Such things, then, were the bad signs.

But fortunately there were also those which gave her hope, signs which without doubt had to be interpreted positively. She liked his habit of rubbing his hand over his eyes when he was concentrating or at breakfast of breaking his bread into two pieces exactly the same size – indeed the way he then took hold of the teapot with both hands could actually make her burst out laughing with relief. She liked the fact that he seldom came home later than he had said – and was equally pleased that he stayed out just as long as he had said. For one thing she was absolutely sure of: even if Thomas's spiritual presence was a precondition for the arrival of the letter, his physical presence was a hindrance –Thomas had to have left home a long time ago if the letter was to reach her.

And little Margaretha?

It was worse with little Margaretha – before very long she realized that all the worst and the most threatening portents in one way or another were connected with her, in actual fact the girl's talk about Wurstelprater (about the visit that naturally had not materialized even though it had been warm enough for a long time) was what she feared most of all. When the little girl with a dreamy expression murmured something about the white swan nowadays she felt a creeping anguish, when the girl smiled she was seized by panic. But since, however, the worst would be if she allowed the girl to realize what was going on inside her she did everything she could to hide her feelings, and the strange (and uncanny) thing was that the girl seemed not to notice the change that had taken place: little Margaretha acted during these weeks as devotedly and confidingly as ever. If anything, Magda sometimes thought, she is even more open, talkative and devoted than before.

Then one evening in the middle of May – in an unexpected and surprising manner – the whole thing came to a conclusion. Thomas had said that he would come home from the hospital by about four o'clock in the afternoon. At eight o'clock in the evening she still hadn't heard from him. By nine o'clock she was beside herself. When he came through the door about half an hour later she already knew that something terrible had happened. Thomas was pale and constrained. He hurried past her into the living-room and sank down on the sofa before even taking off his coat. For a short while he sat hunched, staring vacantly ahead, then he put his hands over his face and burst out crying.

His whole body was racked with sobs. He wept for a long time – loudly and with abandon like a child.

She stared at him in horror.

József? passed through her consciousness. József!

But Thomas's late arrival home and his deep despair had nothing to do with József but with his Uncle Karl. Uncle Karl was dead. He had, she learned later when Thomas had calmed down somewhat, been run over by a tram at Schottentor and had died in the ambulance on the way to the hospital. The funeral was to take place on Sunday, 26 May, in a week's time.

The days that now followed were dream-like and filled with a strangely pale and, as it were, vapid silence in which every individual sound soon swelled up and was distorted beyond recognition. Little Margaretha came as usual on both Monday and Friday, but otherwise nothing was the same. Thomas no longer wept. Nor did he say much. It was really only on that first evening after he had finally ceased sobbing, that he had talked to her about his uncle – for hours he had then in a voice which at regular intervals broke with sorrow, described episodes from his uncle's life: things he himself remembered and things he had heard described. His uncle, he had said, had been so unlike everybody else. And not only in appearance. No, it wasn't only the hump and his ludicrously waddling gait that distinguished him from his surroundings – it was to an equal degree his profound sympathy. Uncle Karl, he had said, was – as well as a much-valued solicitor, not only loved by the clients whose cases he won but also by those whose cases he lost – one of the few in our country who during the war saved Jewish families from annihilation. "My uncle", he had said, "had a friendly disposition. The only time my uncle lost hope", he said, "was during the war when he feared that he would end up in one of the Nazi hospitals for cripples, all of which had the positive consequence for us children", he soon added, "that he too came to live in the isolated village in Burgenland where we had been sent by our father after our mother's death. Uncle Karl", he had then said, "loved beautiful clothes, opera and good food" – and then he had told her (for the umpteenth time) about all the afternoon hours in his childhood spent together with his uncle at Café Landtmann. By the time Thomas finally grew silent they were both exhausted and almost immediately had fallen into a deep sleep. When she awoke the next morning Thomas was already shaved, dressed and, so it seemed, composed ready for the tasks awaiting him – and so from that moment he had barely said a word to her.

Now he spoke only to the relatives and the only topic they discussed was the approaching funeral out at the Central Cemetery, the Zentralfriedhof.. The telephone rang frequently. "My dear little friend," the aunt said if it was Magda who for some reason answered instead of Thomas, "my dear, may I speak to

Thomas!" "My dear little friend," she also said, "you must understand that this is a hard blow for Thomas, he and his uncle were very close". Then she sighed and asked again to speak to Thomas, and if he wasn't in she said she would call back later. "Tell him I called!" she then said – but always without saying why she had rung. Lots of flowers arrived too. The flat was pervaded by a sweet and cloying scent which wouldn't go away no matter how much she aired the place.

Then at last it was Sunday.

The morning was overcast, with a chance of rain. The actual funeral service took place in Dr Karl Luegerkirche within the Zentralfriedhof. One had expected that the church would be filled to bursting point, that masses of friends, colleagues and business acquaintances would have foregathered to follow "this honourable old servant of the law" (as Thomas's father expressed the matter) to his last resting place, but almost half the pews gaped empty and apart from a few outsiders, it was really only the nearest relatives who attended. Even so the whole thing went off with dignity and grandeur. There were masses of flowers, mostly chrysanthemums which together with the incense filled the church with their heavy, sickly sweet smell, there was the coffin: black, shining, beautifully adorned and so huge that one couldn't help thinking about the deformed (and badly disfigured) body hidden within, and there were white lilies which had been placed on the coffin lid like two white hands crossed over a black-clad breast. The addresses were numerous and lengthy. The music was admittedly very splendid but at the same time surprisingly varied for a funeral: there was among other things a performance of a melting aria from Wagner's *Parsifal* which according to Thomas's father had been his brother's favourite opera.

When after almost two hours they left the church the clouds had dispersed, the sun was baking and it was stiflingly hot. The cortège began to move slowly along the main road to the left which like a reminder of eternity stretched in a south-westerly direction as far as the eye could see. Both sides of the road were bordered by tall trees, by deciduous trees, the crowns of which glistened in the sun, and also by different kinds of conifers: dark, gloomy yew-trees, and pruned cypresses, pine trees, larches and junipers; between the trees one could catch a glimpse of grave-yards with their small benches, flowers and huge monuments in granite or marble. A low iron fence marked a clear boundary between the area of the dead and the cemented road where the still living moved forward. The coffin rested on a huge catafalque drawn by two horses with black plumes, first after the coffin came the deceased's brother and sister, after them Thomas, Stefan and Martin. Elise and the two children followed close on their heels. All of them, including the children, were dressed in black down to the smallest button. It was very quiet. The only sound to break the deep silence was the clip-clap of the horseshoes on the cemented road, the rhythmic scraping of many feet and the occasional, quickly suppressed cough. The procession followed the main road up to the first large cross-roads, from which eight equally straight and apparently equally endless roads branched out. Here one took to the left, after a fur-ther hundred yards or so one turned off once more.

Magda walked alone some ten yards from Thomas and his family. She had deliberately drawn back a little, why she didn't rightly know – the only thing that surprised (and hurt) her was that none of the others seemed to have noticed that she had fallen behind. From her place a little to the side of the column, on the other hand, she could see the catafalque better, not least every time the procession changed direction. The catafalque and those following most closely behind it. The brother, the sis-ter and the nephews, Elise, the children and a few more, pre-sumably Thomas's cousins whose names she didn't even know.

When she now observed all these relatives, so doggedly gloomy, so pale and seemingly transparent against all the black, she had to marvel at how different their faces appeared to her – how unlike the faces she had grown used to. And while the procession approached the graveyard at a snail's pace the feeling grew ever stronger within her that in actual fact it was precisely these faces, white and rigid as masks, that were the real ones; indeed, she thought, just as the catafalque stopped and Thomas, his brothers and three of the presumed cousins lifted the coffin on to their shoulders, it was as if only now did she see their true selves – and these selves were completely alien to her!

Alien to me, she also thought, but not to each other.

No, she thought, on the contrary. Among themselves, they are all similar to the point of confusion. United in their sorrow and their memories of the deceased, enclosed in those memories, in all their memories, as in a light circle. A circle of light, she thought, an illuminated scene – to which I myself have no entry.

The thought made her feel slightly giddy.

But she also felt something resembling shame.

Yes, she really did feel ashamed – but despite that (or perhaps just because of it?) she couldn't force herself to hurry to catch up with them at last. At the graveside too she held herself slightly behind the others. When it was time to go forward to take a final farewell of the deceased she kept a few more paces behind. She hesitated for a moment and cast a shy glance around her – before letting the white rose that someone had handed to her fall to the ground. Soon afterwards it was all over. They returned to the main entrance. Now too Magda held back, but nobody seemed to miss her now either – not even Thomas. The cars were waiting on the open space outside the wall. She saw Thomas helping his father into the first car and immediately afterwards, to her surprise, getting into the back seat of the car himself. For a moment she didn't know what she should do, in which car she was now expected to travel, and suddenly without having time to think about it, she waved little Erich over to her, bent down and whispered in his ear that when the cars arrived at Canovagasse he was to tell Thomas that she had developed a terrible headache and instead of going with the others had taken a tram straight home. "Tell Thomas," she murmured, straightening up and casting a furtive glance around her, "that I haven't the least desire to have dinner at Canovagasse, but that he's free to stay as long as he likes". Then she withdrew cautiously backwards towards the entrance until she could disappear unobserved through the gate. Once in the shelter of the wall she stopped and caught her breath before, half-running and afraid that someone might even now come for her, she made for the nearest gate, gate number three, which was only a few hundred yards from the main entrance.

Back out on Simmeringer Hauptstrasse she boarded the waiting tram and sat down on one of the vacant seats right at the back of the carriage. Suddenly she was neither ashamed nor in despair – she was furious. While the tram clattered back towards the centre of the town rage boiled within her, the most bitter and rancorous thoughts swirled around in her head, in fact the closer the tram came to Schwarzenbergplats the more she became filled with hatred. With a violent and unreasonable hatred. A hatred with a strength she had hitherto not believed she was capable of. She hated everything about these relatives, about Thomas too, hated their self-assurance, their rapid speech, and their wit, she hated the sudden changes in their conversations, the insinuations, their knowing smiles with which they accompanied their phrases, the incomprehensible, and perhaps just for that reason unassailable blend of passion and total indifference – and most of all she hated their laughter.

Their laughter which in some peculiar manner always seemed to be directed just at her. Which always seemed to mark a dividing line between them and her, a wish to efface her, perhaps even more to render her harmless, rather like protecting oneself against moth damage with a light squirt. Oh, those laughs, she thought just as the tram braked at the tram stop, those ghastly, ugly, insidious laughs – how I hate them.

Now the tram rolled on again.

And why don't they ever talk about Hungary? she thought. Why have they completely stopped talking about what is happening in Budapest or Sopron or for that matter along the borders of Burgenland? Oh, she thought, and now she was close to tears, it's their fault.

Everything's their fault!

It's their silence that eroded my dreams and my memories. Yes, she thought, surprised at how well it all fitted, since they never ask a single word about my past it doesn't exist either. I disturb them, she thought in amazement at the very moment the tram arrived at Schwarzenbergplatz, I remind them of something they would never for the life of them want to be reminded about. She allowed the crowd to carry her out of the carriage and away towards the tram stop on the Ring. After waiting a few minutes she was seized by impatience and began to walk quickly instead along the avenue in the direction of Schottentor. When she had come here at first, she seemed to remember, she had experienced their silence rather as a relief, as an invitation to participate, in fact as a kind of openness. Now she knew suddenly that all that was an illusion. Merely a game. As false as everything else they applied themselves to.

And now, she thought bitterly, it's all too late as well.

To start now to talk about the past would seem strange, if she were now to drag out information about her mother, about her life in Brennbergbánya, about the school or even about her escape, they would only find her ludicrous and ridiculous. And anyway, she thought as she passed the Burgtheater, I no longer have anything to relate. No, she thought a little later as she sat down in the tram on the way to Gersthof, there's really nothing left that I'd be able to tell them. Nothing, she thought – and again was suffused with a feeling of guilt, such a strong feeling

of having betrayed all those people and all those places that had
once been so close to her, that at that moment she would have
liked nothing better than to sink through the ground and disappear. On arriving home, just as she stepped in through the archway in Hockegasse, she met the caretaker and the two
neighbours' wives, all three deeply involved in a discussion
which obviously concerned a storm of protest of some sort, a
campaign which the press was said to have started up against
the radio; they were talking loudly and eagerly and kept interrupting each other, especially the caretaker who was bright red
in the face and didn't seem to have noticed that his little black
beret had slipped off and landed on the ground. When Magda
went past they fell silent – all at the same time and as if at a given
signal. Only when she had closed the outer door behind her
could she hear how the discussion had started up again.

When she hung up her black coat in the hall she noticed that
the clock in the living-room showed seven o'clock. She went out
into the kitchen and drank a glass of water, then stood a long
time, staring with unseeing eyes at the black tin roof on the other
side of the courtyard. Since she didn't know what she should do
with herself she went and lay down. Remarkably enough she
drifted almost immediately into an agreeable semi-stupor –
Dagmar Fuhrich passed through her fuddled consciousness just
before she fell asleep, it's exactly the same with me as with Dagmar Fuhrich: it's the same forces that have killed us both.

Dagmar Fuhrich was also the first thought to come to her when
she awoke the next morning – but now she couldn't for the life of
her understand what the poor ballet girl's death had to do with
her herself. She knew, on the other hand, that if the letter from
József didn't arrive in the next few days she would be forced to
ask Thomas for help – despite everything it was her only chance.

Thomas had come home late from the funeral dinner. She
had woken when he crept into the bed, had expected him to say

147

something, but when he didn't do so she hadn't asked either. Now in the morning too he was silent, he appeared abstracted in a way she had never noticed earlier in him and he complained about a headache – something in his manner told her however that his melancholy came about not only from his headache or grief over his uncle but had other causes too. Later in the day when he gave an – admittedly brief – account of the previous day's dinner at Canovagasse she became convinced that during the course of the evening something had been played out between Thomas and his father, something unexpected and perhaps decisive – and in any event something of a nature that Thomas now didn't want to discuss with her.

But then what does it matter that he doesn't say anything? she thought. The only thing of significance now is the letter.

But why, she thought several days later, why doesn't he tell me what he has dreamt? Yes, she asked herself, why has he never ever told me about his dreams?

They were now already into June.

"Where have you been? she asked when he came home in the evenings later than he had said. "And what were you and Martin really talking about on the 'phone yesterday evening, when you thought I was asleep?"

She looked at him challengingly when he sat at the other side of the table, with his back to the window.

He met her gaze, then he laughed.

"Oh," he said, "it was no doubt one of the usual arguments about von Karajan. Martin considers him to be a genius, just as father does, they can't feel how limited he actually is, how his cold perfectionism makes him a pure charlatan."

He lit a cigarette, drew on it deeply and let the smoke slowly filter through his nose.

"No, come to think of it," he then said, "we didn't talk about von Karajan but about Semmelweis. Martin wants me to write an article on Semmelweis, it will soon be a hundred years since he died. Semmelweis worked for many years at the General Hospital, the Allgemeines Krankenhaus, admittedly as a gynaecologist but anyway on the same premises as we're now using."

He then laid his head against the wall and closed his eyes.

So, four weeks after the funeral, four weeks during which she had hardly seen anything of Thomas (when she woke in the morning he had already gone and in the evenings he had come home late, so late that she had often gone to sleep, and if she even so had been awake and asked him where he had been he had always answered the same thing: that there was a lot to do at the clinic and that he had now started his research around Semmelweis's personality), after four weeks except for two days (this was on a Friday) the letter finally came – she found it in their letter-box when she returned home after strolling around in town aimlessly all morning. For a moment everything went black before her eyes. Then she pulled herself together, and with the letter pressed to her, went hesitantly up the stairs, unlocked the door and hurried over to the writing desk in the living-room where she found the thin silver paperknife she had bought for Thomas's birthday several years ago. Her hand trembled as she carried the knife to the letter. It was only when she began to slit the envelope that she noticed that there was something wrong. She turned over and read the back of the envelope. And discovered: this wasn't the letter from József that she was expecting. It was her own letter that had been returned!

She went out into the hall where she sank down on to a chair. Again and again she read what was written. Beside József's name and address which had been crossed out someone had written in a foreign language (and in red ink) four words which she realized meant that the addressee was unknown and that the letter was to be returned. Return to sender, she thought in confusion, that must be what it says there. Return to sender? She stared at the text unable to understand.

Who has written it? she thought.

And why, she thought, have they prevented him from receiving my letter?

Then – at the very moment the clock in St Leopoldskirche struck two – the doorbell rang. She gave a start and stared in horror at the door. O God, was the first thought that entered her mind, it's locked, isn't it? Then she waited, motionless.

It was silent out there.

After a minute or two it rang again, a short and peremptory signal this time – then it was silent again. Her heart was pounding in her breast. As if paralysed she stared at the handle, tried to stop breathing, somehow to prevent betraying her presence.

Only after an endlessly long while could a third ring be heard.

Immediately after that a knocking – first one, and then another considerably more cautious than the first.

Finally – a whisper: "It's me…Margaretha…"

Has she heard me? she thought at the same moment that the sound of a sob penetrated through to her. Does she know that I am at home?

But then, just as the sob seemed to develop into crying she finally heard the light scraping of footsteps receding – and it really was silent at last. Even so it was a few more minutes before she dared to get up from the chair and – still with pounding heart and bated breath – to steal out into the hall and into the bedroom. She spent the rest of the day huddled up in bed, in a kind of semi-stupor. Towards evening she thought she noticed that Thomas had come home, but she didn't know if she had really just imagined it. Gradually she fell asleep.

And now she heard them again – the voices. They whirled round in the darkness surrounding her, in the darkness where she too hovered, so strangely and frighteningly weightless. They swept towards her, clammy and cold, changed into giggles and protracted, half-smothered laughs. "Moosbrugger," it was a whisper (but why could nobody explain who that Moosbrugger was?) "My dear little friend," she heard the aunt's voice, "my dear"; soon Elise giggled and murmured the repulsive rhyme about stabs and blood. She mumbled about little girls and about the murderer always having chubby hands with short, dough-white fingers. But at that moment there was another voice too. A child's voice: light and clear and knife-sharp – and in a dizzyingly fast movement she was hurled up out of the darkness. She gasped. For a fraction of a second she thought she could hear the sound of a baby crying – then finally it was silent. A pale light shone through the curtains, grey, distorting: at the first moment she was not sure where she was. Then she heard the voice again.

József?

What did he want of her? And how had he managed to get here on his own? Oh, it passed through her mind, József is calling me.

It's time! she thought. Now I must go to him.

3

And so she went to him.

She got up, went unobserved over to the chair where her clothes lay, changed from her nightgown into a dress, slipped out through the door and closed it silently behind her. József, she thought as she sneaked out through the outside door, carefully turned the key in the lock and with a hesitant gesture popped it into her dress pocket. József, she thought, don't be uneasy, I'm coming now – and then she hurried down the two flights of stairs and out through the door. She stopped for a moment in the courtyard, overwhelmed by the pregnant silence – by the silence and by the shadows that seemed to lurk out there in the semi-darkness. She looked around her in confusion. Then she slipped through the archway out on to the street – but only to stop once more. The street too lay deserted. Apart from a vague rustling from the dustbin there wasn't a sign of life.

And where was she to go now? Should she turn off down towards Gersthof or should she follow Hockegasse up towards the residential area?

Where was he leading her?

And why was he hiding from her out there somewhere in the darkness?

At that moment she heard a slight scraping sound, like a footstep. Oh, she laughed, of course! – and so she hurried up

Hockegasse, turned off to the left at the first crossing and continued in the direction of St Leopoldskirche. It was pitch black in the park round the church. The gravel was damp and cold under her feet. But she mustn't hesitate now. With her heart pounding with excitement she managed to get over to the football pitch; when she found it deserted she let her searching gaze roam over the empty benches, tried to discern whether there was, all the same, somebody moving in the shadow of the trees, if there was some sign to decipher, some hint as to the direction in which he now wanted her to continue.

Then she heard it again!

Yes, there it was again, the slight scraping of feet – but now from over beside the church itself. Relieved she sought her way over there. József, she whispered quietly to herself, little József! Oh, it was so wonderful that he was finally back! How happy she was! Happy and filled with gratitude! But look! – now almost unnoticed he had in the strictest privacy led her round the church, up Bastiengasse and past the Semmelweis clinic.

In a kind of semi-circle?

But – what was the street in which she now actually found herself?

How alien everything suddenly seemed.

József, she thought, where have you really led me to?

Dürwahringstrasse – was this in actual fact the viewpoint in Dürwahringstrasse? How had she got there in that case? And what was the significance of the iron railings? The valley glimpsed down below and the grass that rubbed so damply against her bare legs?

József?

Why have you sent that elder bush in my way – and why is it already flowering, with such unnaturally white flowers?

She listened out in the darkness, tried to strain her hearing to the limit.

József? she whispered again.

Then she moved around quickly, suddenly terrified that he was already on the point of leaving. With wildly beating heart she ran in the direction she assumed that Bastiengasse ought to lie, if I only hurry, she thought, if I only hurry I shall find him before everything is too late. But no, the houses were transformed while she ran: they changed their shape, were distorted, slipped away – and in a vacuum she fumbled, in a black and damp vacuum where nothing could any longer by discerned.

And then she heard it.

His laughter! A wicked laugh: scornful and without pity!

Oh, she thought, confused, I ought to have understood – and unresisting allowed herself to sink back into the darkness.

STEINHOF

As if from an endless distance the words penetrated her darkness.

Light, impossible to defend oneself against.

"From where I'm standing here by the window I can glimpse the town, far down there – sparkling and unreal in the sun haze."

Thomas's voice, yes, it really was his voice – but it sounded so odd, rough and strangely hoarse.

"I can see the nearest pavilions of the hospital complex... two intersecting roads, a few benches, rows of trees...something like a patch of grass down below here where some figures dressed in white are busy playing football."

Football? flashed through her subconscious. Football?

She wished he would go away

"The church" (oh, why wouldn't he leave her in peace),"on the other hand, I can't see the church. Nor the pavilions over on Baumgartnerhöhe – because the trees are far too high and the vegetation far too dense for that."

Then he did fall silent. The words released their grip on her and – finally! – she could let herself sink back into the darkness.

Into that gentle, refreshing, cotton-wool-soft darkness.

But then: a movement, sudden and alarming.

And now, there he was again all the same, right next to her. Close – just far too close.

She could feel rather than see him: seemed to discern that he had his arms folded over his chest and that he was trying incessantly to catch her eye.

And what was it that he was actually talking about?

His voice sounded so strange, she thought, as if strained through an invisible filter: he wanted, she heard him say, he wanted her to understand why he had waited so long before visiting her.

"If you're at all aware of how much time has elapsed since you were admitted here."

Admitted ?

Admitted here?

He wanted her to know, he said, that the reason for his delay was that the ward doctor was adamantly opposed to his visit.

"It proved impossible to persuade him."

But now, he said, after a long discussion with the consultant instead, he'd been given permission to come when and as often as he pleased.

He fell silent, cleared his throat.

Then he murmured something about the catatonic state she had slipped into being considered by the doctors here at Steinhof as a state of total – withdrawal. That the immobility, the passivity, indeed the "deathlike status" in which her body now found itself, was a kind of voluntary act. That she had thus chosen to shut herself in. To shut herself in and let the world remain outside. That it was of her own free will that she now, according to these same doctors, couldn't understand a word he said.

"Free will!" – it was as if he spat the words out.

"Rubbish!" Heavens, why couldn't he just leave her be?

"I refuse to believe them! Catatonia, hypokinaesia, stupor – what is it except words and labels. Simplifications. Blinkers and the need to control.

"A subtle way of exercising power.

"And," he said, "it's something that makes me furious".

He was silent for a while.

"No", he then said, "even if you appear dead to the world around you, I know you can hear me. I know that you're listening. That you're listening. And...

"and for God's sake..."

But now his voice suddenly rose to a scream: "...for God's sake, Magda, answer me!"

Was he actually burying his head in his hands?

"Magda," he whispered.

For a moment it sounded as though he was crying.

Then at last it was silent.

The darkness lightened a little, clatter, shadows.

Strange voices.

But – among them too (naturally, as always nowadays) his. Yes, now he was sitting on the edge of her bed again: she thought she could almost smell his breath, a sourish smell that reminded her of something – of something she had forgotten.

"Forgive me for what happened yesterday."

For what happened yesterday?

"I shan't get carried away again." He was whispering now. And he touched her   indeed at the very moment the words reached her she could also feel how he brushed her cheek with his fingertips.

Oh, if only she weren't so tired – if she could only bring herself to open her mouth and shout at him to go away.

To let her be, at last.

"You're so cold," he continued. "Your cheek's like ice. And yet it's warm here next to the window. Warm – or at least light.

"Your window faces north-east," he added after a while. "So you get the morning sun. As opposed to the others." It seemed as if he was nodding towards the row of beds further into the ward, "since all those alongside the windows face north.

"It's so quiet in here," he said, thoughtfully. "You could imagine they were all asleep with their eyes open" – and it seemed to her suddenly as if his voice not only came from a long way away: it was as if he existed in another world, separated from her by an invisible membrane. A membrane of light.

"You're not only cold," now the words were there again. "You're also unnaturally pale."

Then they fell silent all the same.

Was he hesitating?

No, he was continuing now – although hesitantly, as if half to himself. The strange thing was, he said, that despite her inaccessibility, indeed despite the fact that her silence struck him as both alien and aloof, she was so desirable.

Desirable?

Now he took her hand, too. Indeed he bowed over it, he kissed it and remained sitting with her hand thus pressed firmly against his lips for a long time, before suddenly (as if frightened) flinging it back down on to the blanket. Then he really did get up off the bed. He hesitated slightly – but no, instead of leaving he went over to the window: she seemed to realize that he was leaning his forehead against the pane and that his shoulders were shaking as if he was weeping.

Then everything grew quiet, dark. Until his voice groped its way into her again.

"Today too", she heard him whisper, "today too they're playing football down there on the grass."

He took a deep breath.

"The referee", he then said, in a voice that was firmer than before, "is sitting in a wheelchair. The boy," he continued, "the poor lad can't be any more than sixteen or seventeen at the most, has nothing on except a white knee-length shirt. His bare legs and feet are whitish grey and as lean as gnawed chicken wings, he has his locker key hanging from a red ribbon round his neck, and when he lifts his arm to blow the whistle, for he's got a whistle, the drip sways like a reed in the wind".

Here she seemed to notice that he was bending forward and shielding his eyes with his hand. Before he sat up straight again.

"It's so quiet in the flat at Hockegasse," he then said. "The silence is really often more than I can bear.

If she only knew what he wanted of her.

Why he was so persistent.

All she wanted, after all, was to be left in peace.

To be allowed to remain here in the darkness.

"Magda."

Now he was talking to her again, whispering. She even imagined she could feel the slight touch of his lips against her ear: "Magda, come back!"

Then followed a moment's silence.

"Your pallor" – and now, it suddenly seemed to her, it was as if the actual words had become lips, as if they were groping over her face, clammy, warm and intrusive – "your pallor frightens me".

Oh, if only he would leave her alone.

"I can't understand it," he added.

Then she noticed that he had got up.

That he had got up and gone over to his place at the window.

"Oddly enough," she heard after a while, "oddly enough it's easier to talk with you…

…or," he amended, "to you…– when I am standing here by the window and looking out, than when I sit so close".

Yes, he continued (and it was a relief that he was speaking from over there now), when he saw one of the white-clad figures go past down below on the gravel path, "oh, and there's one person just now who's wearing striped pyjamas with absurdly large trousers, so he has to hold them up with one hand the whole time," when he saw these poor creatures moving like shadows among the tall tree trunks, when he saw the leafy treetops and the thin wisps of cloud above them he not only found it easier to endure her silence – he also knew then with certainty that she was listening.

Perhaps he knew it with such certainty, he said, because here by the window he could see her so clearly before him.

He could see how she turned towards him, he said, how she smiled and how sometimes she even nodded at his words in agreement. She was there so clearly before his eyes, hovering half-transparent in the sun haze over the town – just as simultaneously, and now it almost sounded as if he were smiling himself, she was, in the most wonderful and paradoxical way, so alive and attentively listening where she lay in the white hospital bed behind his back.

After that a long silence ensued.

"Here comes the young football referee now, driving like a madman in his wheelchair down there," he said at last. "The sun has gone behind a cloud and in fact the grass is already shining with moisture."

Oh, this shapeless darkness.

Rising, falling, always in motion.

"My aunt rang yesterday," he said – and for a moment everything went quiet.

"Aunt…" he said.

And she let it be.

"Aunt was so obsessed with the death of the pope," he said, "especially with his difficult and protracted death throes. And as usual she dwelt throughout the whole of the conversation on everything except what we were both thinking about."

That, he said softly while slowly and abstractedly rubbing his hand over the window pane, that in fact was something his aunt had done ever since John XXIII had died at the beginning of June.

Yesterday, he continued, she had at first talked long and ardently about the dead pope and then at least as long about the new one who was to be elected the day after tomorrow, she had talked about the weather prospects for next weekend, a heat-wave was said to be on the way, and finally, in fact in the same breath as she had suggested that he should go out to Nussdorf as soon as Friday, she had lowered her voice and in the most confidential tones begun to whisper about the latest jealousy homicide – about a man who had stabbed his neighbour to death at twenty-seven Malfattigasse.

"Aunt...", he said.

"It's really just like my aunt"– but at that moment his voice broke into a sob.

After a while, she saw, he let his fingertips glide slowly over the glass, over the window frame where the white paint was peeling and finally, in an almost caressing gesture, over the thin bars over the lower panes. "But before I go out to Nussdorf..." here he was silent again, as if he had forgotten what he had intended to say, and there was a long pause before he said anything more. "Before I go there," he then murmured, "I shall visit Dr Erna Lesky."

Then he continued with a slightly incoherent explanation that Dr Lesky was head of the institute for medical history at Josephinum, that just now she was working on a book on Semmelweis and that it was said that no one had such a knowledge of the scandalous treatment of Semmelweis's discovery as she had. That incidentally there was a lot to do at the clinic. That they feared that the polio outbreak in Budapest was going to spread to Vienna. And that the boy who lacked immune defences was getting worse every day that passed: the poor child could no longer eat, his mouth was one big sore, and there was even thick, viscous mucus running out of his ears.

"It's terrible to watch him suffer," he said. And then: "Forgive me – I ought to talk about something more pleasant, of course."

165

Again, he began his fumbling.

Oh yes, yesterday something had happened to him. Something – "quite funny". He had, he said – in a strange, almost wavering voice – he had gone into the large bookshop in Kärtner Strasse and asked for literature on Semmelweis. "Semmelweis?" the woman assistant had wondered. "Semmelweis – is that the name of a circus?" He had then explained, he said, that Ignaz Philipp Semmelweis was the name of the famous doctor in Vienna who in the mid-nineteenth century discovered that women died in childbirth after they had been infected by something he called corpse poison, a poison that the doctors carried with them from the post-mortem rooms to the maternity clinic. He had then pointed out to the assistant that Semmelweis was a genius but that he was before his time, that he was opposed by everyone and that he ended his life insane. But then, insulted, she had with a toss of her head replied that of course she knew who Ignaz Philipp Semmelweis was, that she had simply misheard the name but that unfortunately, she was quite sure, they didn't have any books about him. "Semmelweis," she had asked as he was leaving, "Semmelweis – wasn't he a Jew?" Something that proved, he said with a short laugh that she was not only ignorant but prejudiced too.

"Incidentally," he suddenly added, "I shan't have time to visit Dr Lesky, I suppose, there's far too much to do at the clinic. I think I'll ring instead."

He rubbed his hand over his eyes.

"I haven't had time to shave, he murmured abstactedly. "I wanted to come here as early as I could."

"Well…" here he broke off.

"The town", he then said, but now his voice broke and he began to cry, wild and unrestrained.

It was only after a long while that he pulled himself together again.

"I'm sorry," he then whispered.

"I know you can hear me," he also said – and she seemed to notice that he was drumming his fingers impatiently on the glass.

"I know…"

At that moment he turned his back to the window and went up to her bed.

"…I know you're listening to every word I say."

And he took her hand.

"It's as if you were hesitating", he said, "as if you hadn't really decided how far you want to follow me."

And now he also bent over her, so that his face was very close to hers.

"Don't be afraid," he breathed against her cheek.

"There's nothing out there to be afraid of."

"Today," he said, "it's more than a week since I visited you the first time."

And she soon heard it : his voice was changed. He not only spoke more quickly than before, almost stumbling over his words – his voice had also something subduing about it, something dogged, almost as if he had made a decision and as if he had resolved to follow it up at any price.

Nor could she help listening.

He had, he said, now standing there by the window with his back to the ward and his eyes gazing into the distance, yesterday he had had a telephone conversation with Dr Lesky.

"A remarkable conversation," he said.

She waited.

Dr Lesky, he said, hadn't behaved as he'd thought she would. Admittedly she had been very polite and obliging – but mostly she'd sounded like a strict teacher chastising a troublesome pupil, in fact when she'd started the conversation by questioning him on what he actually knew about "the young Dr Semmelweis" she'd sounded so harsh that to his surprise he soon found himself rattling off data like a lesson learnt by heart. "Born 1818 in Buda, doctorate in Vienna 1844, assistant at the obstetric clinic at the Allgemeines Krankenhaus from 1846, refused extension of his appointment 1849, as a consequence of which he returned to Budapest 1850, served at St Rockhaus hospital, married, two children, opposed by all his contemporaries and died in a mental hospital in Vienna 1865..." – here she'd interrupted him, had laughed, almost embarrassed, and excused herself by saying that she hadn't meant to sound rude.

"You could hear," he said, "that she was reflecting".

Then he paused slightly, as if he was wondering about something, perhaps about the real content of that reflection. "Then," he went on, "she wanted to know what had interested me in Semmelweis's fate in the first place. I said that my brother had asked me to write an article for his periodical, but that I also found Semmelweis's case extraordinarily shocking. 'Shocking,' she said. 'Perhaps complicated too?' Now I was the one to laugh: 'More shocking than complicated really,' I admitted. 'There's nothing strange about academic disputes in themselves, of course.' 'You find it shocking that his colleagues could be so obdurate, narrow-minded and unintelligent?' she wondered, and now she sounded positively friendly. 'And greedy for power naturally,' I answered. 'Naturally they were afraid that they'd be overtaken by a younger and more gifted talent, by a person who, what's more, was an outsider.' 'You see the whole thing as a struggle for power between the reactionary Professor Klein and the young gifted Semmelweis? she wondered further. 'Naturally', I said, 'the whole thing makes me furious.'

"When she didn't comment on that in any way, I explained further that I couldn't deny that I did have difficulty in understanding how even a lust for power could make not only Klein but practically all his contemporaries so blind that they couldn't even see the very concrete results of Semmelweis's experiments, 'despite everything the number of deaths did fall drastically as soon as the doctors followed his advice and washed their hands in a chlorine solution after the post-mortems.' 'Come here at four o'clock on Thursday of next week,' she then said, 'on 27 June. I should very much like to show you all the hitherto unknown material that I've just been going through.' Then she fell silent, I waited. 'I've absolutely nothing against your referring to my research in your article,' she declared at last. After that she ended the conversation without even saying goodbye.

"I must admit," he said, "I really must admit that I'm curious. As far as I can see the case of Semmelweis is as clear as day- it's shocking and cruel, but even so there's not much to wonder about.

"What's more," he murmured – but now he suddenly lost the thread and began instead to walk back and forth across the floor. "What's more..." The refracted rays of the sun shone on his back, it was already warm in the ward, almost stifling. He walked in the sunlit square in front of the window, turned each time for some reason just before stepping from the rectangle of light into the shade. He kept his arms crossed, his white coat flapped round his legs – "and incidentally," he murmured, "it ought to interest you. Semmelweis was from Hungary after all. And he too felt...misunderstood".

Then he suddenly stopped in the middle of a stride, turned and instead came and sat down on the edge of her bed.

"Magda," he said imploringly, "I just don't understand...!"

Then he broke off again.

"If you could at least look at me," he continued. "Do you remember? The sweet-smelling stocks are in flower now and the evenings are just as still and warm as that time."

"Magda," he whispered, "you used to say..."

Then he stood up quickly.

Explained that it was Saturday today, that it looked like being a hot day and that he now intended to go directly out to Nuss-dorf. That he would stay there overnight and so he wouldn't be able to come back before tomorrow evening, some time round about seven at the very earliest.

Then he turned and hurried out of the ward.

It was very quiet after he had gone. A thrill of terror passed through her – then she sank back again into the darkness.

The next time he had flowers with him, white stocks which he placed beside her pillow.

If only she weren't so tired.

And they smelt so strong. So sweet and cloying.

But now he was already sitting on the edge of her bed.

"I remember when I saw you for the first time," she heard his voice. "You were so unlike all the others, so irresistibly – alien."

He took her hand.

There was another thing too, he said, something that he had gone and thought about: her aversion to the words "I under-stand". It was, he said, while seeming to play with her fingers absentmindedly, it was as if she had detested those very words from the first moment.

Yes, really, when he thought more about it, he was quite sure that she didn't only detest them – she was afraid of them. It was, he said, as if she didn't fear anything so much as his under-standing. He remembered that she used to smile when he pointed out how well he understood her, but how her eyes at the same time grew dark and dismissive – indeed melancholy. And once, which he remembered only too well, she had shouted at him that he was lying, that he was lying to her and that he was lying to himself, and that in fact he understood nothing. He also remembered, he said, that he'd been deeply wounded – hurt and furious – and that he soon afterwards had left in a rage.

Here he stopped, as if he didn't rightly know how to continue.

"Now," he then said, "now I believe that it's beginning to dawn on me what you meant." He began to realize, he explained while seeming to be groping for the right words, he had begun to realize more and more clearly that while there was still time, in his eagerness to have already understood – perhaps it was his longing for closeness that had deceived him – he had quite forgotten to ask some questions.

He squeezed her hand hard.

Then he let go of it quickly, got up from the bed and went over to the window.

"It's already growing dark," he said, "there's not a soul to be seen down there in the park". And now he let his fingers trace along the window frame, their habitual circular movements, over the peeling specks, down along the white bars and back again.

He cleared his throat slightly.

"Oh," he murmured, "if I only knew…"

He sighed deeply, leant against the window mullions and put his hands deep down into the pockets of his white coat.

"Oh," he said, "of course I ought to have understood how to ask the right questions.

"The right questions…?"

Then he was silent.

It was only after a long while that he began to speak again.

"Yesterday evening," he then said, and now he sounded not only dogged as he had done several times earlier, he also sounded slightly surprised, "yesterday evening, when I was about to go to sleep, something very unexpected happened to me".

She waited, suddenly filled with something that most of all resembled anticipation.

And he continued.

He explained that the day out at Nussdorf had been tiring and that he had gone to bed early. That his aunt had made up a bed for him in his old room, "in the attic, you know, that blue room just under the tin roof where my brothers and I used to live during the summer weeks we always spent with our aunt, while our mother was still alive". It was, he related, stiflingly hot in the room, the dusk and darkness hadn't cooled it down in the least. The window that looked out on to the garden was open and the flowering stocks filled the room with their strong, sweet scent. Only the occasional sound entered from outside: a vague sighing of the trees' foliage, sometimes a branch that creaked or a dog that barked far away. Otherwise silence reigned, a silence so deep that it had made him feel oppressed. "But all at once," he said, and now he suddenly sounded a little more uncertain, "I don't know how to describe it to you, all at once it was as if something had been opened up inside me, as if what just before had seemed alien to me had become something familiar: in a fraction of a second I found myself transported back to the summer evenings of my childhood and I felt rather than remembered how Mother would stand there in the centre of the room, motionless and listening" – he didn't know, he said hesitantly, if he had told her that their mother always used to steal into their room in the evenings when she thought they were asleep. And now, when he had lain there in his old boy's bed, he had for the first time become properly aware of how much he had really loved those moments, those moments when behind tightly closed eyelids – "the last thing I wanted was for her to realize that I was awake" – he had imbibed her presence with an intensity he never otherwise experienced. How much he really had loved her breathless silence and the fleeting kiss on his forehead with which she had always concluded her brief visits and which he had known usually brought an involuntary smile to his lips – "So I have to wonder if she understood all the same that I was awake and that in fact we both shared that certainty as a secret." A secret that in those moments transformed her into a nocturnal angel, someone simultaneously real and quite unreal – "since I never allowed myself on any single occasion to open my eyes and look at her".

Then, he said, yesterday evening "transported to my childhood summer evenings", he had suddenly felt happy, but also terribly lonely. He had lain awake for a long time. "I didn't fall asleep for several hours," he said, "but I slept uneasily and had a confused and very unpleasant dream about a house which at first glance seemed to correspond in detail to everything you could ever wish for. It was large and beautiful and although it was situated in the centre of town it was surrounded by the most beautiful alpine landscape – but the more rooms I discovered in it, the more it appeared dilapidated, menacing and frightening."

He gave a laugh. "Good heavens," he said, "how – pathetic".

For a short while he was silent. Until he continued, now in a lower voice than before: "But do you know, the fact is that this morning, at breakfast, everyone sitting there at the table seemed changed to me, in some way different from usual."

He didn't really know how to explain to her what he meant. Yesterday, he said, when he had gone out to Nussdorf, in fact the whole of that day and evening, everything had been as usual; he and his father had got into an argument about von Karajan, about how the Übermensch attitude von Karajan excelled in at regular intervals, and which he himself deplored, influenced his music. He was irritated as ever by his father's inconsistent attitude, by his arrogant manner and by his way of bringing arguments to a close with an elegant turn of phrase. Aunt gave them her fine fish soup, her renowned apple tart and two bottles of last year's wine, as usual she talked about everything except what the others were discussing, and as usual, he said, towards evening she got lost in the labyrinths of the most current murder mystery, ending up by drawing a few diffuse parallels, as had become her custom recently, between Musil's famous sex killer Moosbrugger and the as yet unknown murderer of Dagmar Fuhrich. "Do you remember her? The little ballet girl who was murdered at the Opera House in the most brutal manner some time at the beginning of the year." Martin, at least as he remembered it, had devoted all his attention to his new mandolin, Elise had sat quietly, and the children, apparently bored, had swung back and forth in the white hammock. "Stefan wasn't there, did I mention that? I think he's in Burgenland with his pupils, unless he's already gone to Italy, he was going to do that some time this summer, I believe."

Anyway, he explained further, everything had seemed to him so disgustingly familiar and predictable yesterday that he had almost regretted having decided not only to spend the weekend at Nussdorf but also his four weeks' holiday now in July. But then this morning when they were having coffee and eating those poppy-seed rolls that he knew she was particularly fond of ("I shall bring one for you next time I'm there, by the way"), well then, this morning when his father wondered who would like to keep him company at the opera next week, when Aunt asked Elise to pass the egg basket, and when Martin, while urging Elisabeth to sit still and little Erich to stop scratching his midge bites, asked how his Semmelweis article was coming along – "Well, at that moment, it was as if I were seeing them all in a new light."

Suddenly, he said hesitantly, suddenly his father had struck him as being so old. He thought he could discern behind his father's haughty mien, he said, a piteous and almost melancholy tone, his aunt's cares had suddenly filled him with tenderness and the sight of Martin, Elise and the two children with something actually resembling sympathy – and he had been seized with a desire to say something affectionate, to rush up and embrace them all – which naturally he didn't do.

"You can imagine how that would have looked."

But still, he added, when later he had walked alone up in the mountains, when he had climbed the steep paths past the vineyards and through the forest right up to the monastery on Leopoldsberg, he had almost been cheered by the thought that he would soon be meeting his family daily – "Yes, I'm actually now looking forward to those four weeks in July with a certain confidence whereas up till now I've been mostly dreading it…", and in the same breath his voice sank to a whisper: "…Oh Magda – you know I want you to be out there with me, that you…"

He fell silent. Rubbed his hand over his eyes and sighed.

"I long for you," he then murmured, "this is – loathsome…degrading…"

There followed another short hesitation.

Degrading, he continued after a while, but confusing too. He was finding it increasingly difficult, he said, to defend himself against his memories, from all the images of her, in particular their first times together came back to him incessantly, in fact often when his attention relaxed the picture of her face emerged before him, open, happy, smiling, oh, dear God, how well he remembered showing her his places – the view from Leopoldsberg, he said, "Do you remember?" or the solitary paths on Gänzehäufel, the silent slimy green pond and the little wooden bridge where they would stand and talk for hours. "Do you remember the first time you were up at the clinic or when we saw *The Diary of Anne Frank* at the Theater in der Josefstadt?" And now in the evenings, he said, he missed her warmth, the smell of her skin, her hands, lips, hair – "Dear God," he whispered, "I long to touch you, to…" and now his voice broke again. The only thing was, he said, that now when he looked at her, when he saw her lying there in bed, so cool and so inaccessible, "so unnaturally beautiful", he blurted out, and sounded more annoyed than despairing, it was, he said, as if the sight of her there in bed made him afraid – there was something so all too elevated about her, something too magnificent about the clarity which now seemed to encircle her being.

"And your silence," he whispered, "who is it you're thinking about there in the darkness of your silence?

"Who is it that you see?"

"Who was it you were really playing for?" he then asked. "You always seemed so happy when you sat there at the piano, so – concentrated."

He had, he said (and now she again wished that he would go away), he had always believed that she liked to play for him, that her music had been a form of address – "a kind of meeting place beyond words".

Now he was no longer sure. Perhaps, he said in a strangulated voice, he had been mistaken the whole time.

Perhaps the music meant something to her that he had never understood – in fact, he said, perhaps it was…?

…"but why?" he almost yelled, "why didn't you ever say any-thing!"

"Sándor?" he wanted to know – but fortunately he soon stopped himself.

Oh, why couldn't he leave her in peace?

Why…?

"Are you aware" – now his voice was there again, insistent and hard, in fact it seemed to be trembling with suppressed anger – was she aware, he wanted to know, that on several occa-sions, in her sleep but also once even during their love-making, she had whispered the name Sándor?

He hadn't wanted to ask anything, he insisted. But why hadn't she said anything?

"Sándor…", he said – and then fell silent and finally rose from the edge of her bed.

He went over to the window.

Hesitated, drummed his fingers against the glass.

Before he began to relate something, incoherently and pausing frequently, about a telephone call he'd had that morning with a colleague, about the heatwave that already meant their having to save water, and about his now having dreamt about houses several times lately in the night, the dreams were very reminiscent of each other, he said, they always dealt with large houses which at first seemed to be full of possibilities but then soon proved to be semi-dilapidated, always in the same unpleasant ways, – dilapidated and, not least, deserted.

The light? it suddenly struck her. This vague, flickering light…?

Only the latest dream had been different, he said. What he now remembered about it was a huge shiny black-and-white-chequered floor, that his father had been as small as a doll and had had quite a limp body, that Martin ("Do you know, how strange, just Martin") had been furious and shouted at their father, but that he himself had put father on a cupboard and asked him if he remembered his childhood – at which his father, he said, and now he sounded really confused, had burst into a resounding guffaw.

He deliberated.

"Father too," he then said, "has, just like you, always loved Liszt, by the way.

"But", he then added almost in the same breath, "no doubt it wasn't just my understanding you were afraid of, I don't think you liked my urging you to try to forget the past, either.

"I don't know," he said, "perhaps…" then he lost the thread again.

"I don't know…"

He cleared his throat slightly.

"And anyway, I expect you're wondering what I want of you. Why I go on talking to you, even though you never answer anything."

His voice was lowered to a whisper.

"But don't you see, Magda", he uttered, so quietly that it was almost inaudible, "Words – in spite of everything, words are our only chance."

He seemed to hesitate slightly.

Then he murmured something about intending to move out to Nussdorf by tomorrow, that he was thinking of working on his Semmelweis article out there and helping his father in the garden, that naturally he would still continue to visit her during those weeks, but perhaps, considering the long journeys, not every day as now but every other day.

"There are two male nurses sitting down there on the grass," he said finally, "in the shade of the trees. They're drinking beer and eating what look like meat pasties.

"One of them's fanning himself with a newspaper.

"The other seems to be on the point of dropping off to sleep the whole time."

Soon after that he left her. As always it was very quiet after he had gone.

And the silence frightened her.

Words?

The thought flickered past like a spark in the darkness.

Words?

At that same moment she heard his voice.

"I moved out to Nussdorf yesterday morning," he said – and she made a real effort to pull herself up to the surface of consciousness.

"It's lovely to get away from the city."

He paused briefly.

"It's lovely to get away from the city," he repeated. "Lovely to know that for four weeks I shall neither need to go back to the clinic nor to our flat, which, I hope you don't mind, I've lent to a research colleague from Australia for the whole of July.

"From Australia…" he murmured abstractedly. Then he got up from the edge of her bed and went over to the window.

She waited.

Oh, she was there now, prepared to follow him, to follow what he said.

"Yes," he said, "It was with a feeling of genuine relief that I got off the bus, and when carrying my suitcase, I walked along the little village road, and when I heard the hens cackling, smelt the scent from the flowering hawthorn and could see from a distance the small turrets on Aunt's house sticking up out of the foliage, I was suddenly seized with contradictory feelings like that night some time ago if you remember, that night when I imagined so clearly that I could feel my mother's presence, or perhaps just as much her absence. The sun was still not very high in the sky, the trees cast long shadows over the road, the vineyards gleamed green up towards the slopes.

"Aunt had laid tea out in the garden," he said – and it occurred to her that his words reminded her most of a melody she had once heard, only she couldn't remember when.

"Aunt", he said, "had also got dressed up in a yellow summer dress, pearls round her neck and a large, rather frayed straw hat pulled down over her grey locks. As usual she prattled on about something she had read in that day's *Kurier*, but when I pointed out that everything became her – her hat, the colour of her dress and the white pearls – she suddenly got stuck in the middle of a sentence and looked aside in confusion. And it struck me, something that otherwise I usually never think about, that she had actually been married a very long time ago – I don't even know if I ever mentioned that to you, but Aunt, now that I think about it, has been a widow for more than forty years. She's kept house for my father for nearly twenty years and, ever since my fifteenth birthday has, you might say, stood in for my mother – without my ever really having taken her seriously."

How still – everything was so still within her now, how…

"We had tea in the shade under the apple trees," he continued.

And for a short, dizzying moment she imagined she could almost smell the vague scent of mint and sun-dried gravel.

"Father", he said, "assured me again and again how pleased he was that I had come to stay for a fairly long time. Then he asked, very discreetly and as if incidentally, how you were, but then straightaway assumed a more ordinary tone of voice and wondered, before I had had time to reply, if I had any idea where Stefan was: if Stefan was still in Burgenland or if he'd returned to Vienna. I told him I didn't know which and we left it there."

He paused briefly.

After a while he added that they were used to Stefan taking off without telling any of the family. He had always done so. And then he had always turned up when it suited him, often on the most unexpected occasions, when he had behaved not hostile, no, rather the opposite, but in a manner that nevertheless gave the others in the family a vague feeling of uncertainty – as if in fact he had observed them on the sly or enjoyed himself at their cost.

"At least that's how I've always thought of it'"

Nevertheless, he said, yesterday at tea he had wondered whether to ask his father what he thought about Stefan's perpetual disappearances – but it had been so quiet and peaceful in the garden and his father had pointed to the vines drooping with clusters of grape beyond the kitchen garden with such pride that he had let the whole thing rest.

Mint, passed through her mind, but also something else, perhaps…

"Instead," he said, "instead I mentioned to father, or to them both, my visit to Dr Lesky last Thursday, when Dr Lesky showed me the letters and papers relating to Semmelweis that she had found in the archives".

Perhaps…, she thought, perhaps incense.

"Aunt was particularly interested in Dr Lesky's character, she had heard, she said, so many differing opinions about her that she was now burning with curiosity to hear my view. Was Dr Lesky as unpleasant as some people maintained? I assured her that that was not at all the case, that Dr Lesky at first sight could appear very gruff, that she was obviously an effective and demanding supervisor, but that she could also smile kindly, that her appearance, small, round, curly-haired and with horn-rimmed spectacles, if anything had something rather girlish about it and that when she had murmured with her gaze lost somewhere in the distance and in a half-absent voice something about Semmelweis always having defended women, not only his patients but also the midwives whom he considered better suited to deliver babies than the male doctors and that in women's vulnerability no doubt he recognized his own – well, I assured Aunt, Dr Lesky then spoke in such a distinct and moving way from her own experiences that any opposition one might have had towards her was soon dispelled."

His father, on the other hand, he said, had been more interested in how Dr Lesky explained the opposition to Semmelweis's ideas. Interested, or really irritated, by what he called "the exaggerated speculation surrounding this extremely ordinary academic quarrel". And when his father at the very moment he himself – perhaps rather stubbornly – had objected that in truth it wasn't a matter of the usual academic squabble but of a purely political one, Dr Lesky's material had convinced him of that, well, when his father at the same moment had cast an injured look at him, stretched out for the teapot and silently poured more tea into his own and the aunt's cup but not in his, then he'd got angry and had been lured into giving an extensive, detailed account of his conversation with Dr Lesky.

"One mustn't forget…", he said.

But then suddenly he got stuck.

He gave a cough.

"It's remarkable," he murmured while beginning to dig in the pockets of his white coat, "would I in normal circumstances have told you all this? Good heavens," he murmured obviously irritated by not finding what he was looking for, "Good heavens, why do I believe so surely that you're listening", he gave a whistle and took a packet of cigarettes out of his breast pocket, "Why," he said, shaking a cigarette out, "why am I really so sure of it?"

At the same moment he glanced around quickly, murmured something inaudible and with an impatient gesture popped the cigarette back into the packet.

"Dear God…", he said.

Then he was silent.

It was very quiet in the ward, very light.

A touch of uneasiness brushed past her.

Like a slight giddiness.

Then his voice was there again: "One mustn't forget," she heard him say, and to her relief the words suddenly streamed out of him, "yes, that's more or less how I began – one must not forget that Semmelweis made his discovery and developed it in the years before, during and after the actual revolution". And Klein, he had then continued, Semmelweis's chief, Professor Klein belonged to the conservative wing, which implied that he not only had the greatest misgivings but also pure horror of any changes which could be construed as changing the given order of things – something, he said, he had been very careful to emphasize, that his father was naturally at least as aware of as he himself. Dr Lesky had shown him innumerable documents in which Klein expressed his intention to oppose these younger doctors' demands for reform with every means at his disposal. Reform! – well, he had a feeling that he had repeated the word several times, as if really to establish its significance. For Klein, he had maintained, just as for most of Klein's contemporaries,

stagnation was a good thing, and every little step, really in what-
ever direction, was a step towards the abyss.

For Klein, he had said and now he could hear how angry he
had sounded, for Professor Klein, Semmelweis implied a
demand for new routines, for washing in chlorine, such a step –
his struggle with Semmelweis was therefore in fact a matter of
life or death. Indeed, if Klein were to have given Semmelweis
even the slightest support for his observations, he had said, then
he himself would have lost his foothold in existence. Oh, this
obtuseness, he had then cried, by this time almost in tears of
rage, "this obtuseness makes me furious, this terrible inability
to see beyond the accepted conceptions drives me to the brink
of madness". And what's more, he had added, his father must
think that it wasn't only Semmelweis's ability to generate new
ideas, his creative intellect and his desire to re-examine the old
theories which seemed challenging to his contemporaries, to
the conservative Klein and the whole Viennese establishment, it
was just as much his character!

"Yes, " he repeated," just as much his character!"

He paused for a short while.

"In fact," he then continued, now more hesitantly than
before, "in fact, I explained to father, everything about Semmelweis constituted a provocation. It wasn't only, I maintained,
that Semmelweis was a nationalist, that he was a liberal, in fact
from 1848 a member of the revolutionary academic legion at the
University of Vienna, it wasn't only that with his straightfor-
ward, impulsive nature he never knew how to behave in accor-
dance with society's unwritten laws, that he was extremely
ascetically inclined in a Vienna that loved to see itself as a hedo-
nistic paradise, or even, as I say, often took women's part rather
than men's – he was, moreover, I explained, Hungarian."

"A Hungarian," he now said. "A Hungarian and therefore –
someone who didn't belong."

He hesitated.

"Semmelweis," I pointed out to father, "spoke German with an accent and he remained all his days a stranger in this country which was nevertheless partly his own.

"Although", he said, "when I had got that far in my comments Aunt hurried to hand me the cake dish."

He leant his head against the window frame. For a while he sat silently and stared out of the window, then he rubbed his hand over his eyes in a weary gesture.

"Father snorted on the other hand," he continued in a low voice after that – so low that it suddenly seemed to her as if he was talking mostly to himself.

"Father wondered if I'd finished.

"Certainly not, I burst out, what makes me so furious..." – and then, he said, his father had in his most restrained tone spoken long and in detail about scientific objectivity and in cases like these the necessity of remaining factual, neutral and impartial, whilst he himself, "in a considerably more excited voice" had given an account of Semmelweis's discovery of corpse poison. He had, he said quietly – and now it was as if he had completely forgotten that she was there behind him – he had stubbornly maintained, while he bent over the table several times to emphasize the importance of his words, that the fact that, despite the incontrovertible evidence of the correctness of Semmelweis's theories, they had refused to listen to him only proved the depth of the conservative dulling of the intellect and showed that they quite simply couldn't accept that an illness like puerperal fever, which was generally considered to be a purely gynaecological illness, indeed even a punishment of the gods directed towards female sexuality, could also strike a man. And most of all he had, he said, repeatedly shouted at his father that the latter understood nothing and that it hadn't, goodness knows, been a question of objectivity but of narrow-mindedness, fear and – pure cowardice.

At which point, he said, Aunt had given a rather forced laugh while his father snorted again and he himself, he'd been so worked up that he had been forced to get up from the table and start walking back and forth between the apple tree and the white hammock, and had shouted that Semmelweis in fact had been nothing other than a Promethean figure – a challenger not only of temporal power but of the divine order too.

Here he stopped for a while to consider.

"But then", he continued, "while I heard my own voice and saw the shadows move almost imperceptibly on the grass in front of my feet, it suddenly struck me that the exchange of opinion between father and me, even though it had had nothing to do with von Karajan this time, resembled all our previous quarrels in the most minute detail. And I was seized," he said, at least that was how he now remembered it, "I was seized with uncertainty, indeed, all at once I was uncertain whether my violent and impotent rage really concerned the aversion to new thinking and openness which had befallen Semmelweis – or actually my father."

So, he said, he had straight away sat down at the table again, and when Aunt had asked him if he would like some more tea, he had held out his cup gratefully. To his surprise Father hadn't seemed willing to continue the conversation either, instead he had been silent for a while and, after they'd finished their tea, he asked if they could go to inspect the vineyards together – "if the weather held" – they would yield a better harvest than for many a year. And several hours later, he said (a sudden tiredness had made his father postpone their walk until the afternoon), a few hours later his father had then led him to his vineyards, where with ill-concealed pride he had shown not only the vineyards but the kitchen garden and the roses. But then, he said, on their way back to the house he had noticed to his surprise that his father was limping slightly, something he had never done before, and this unexpected sign of frailty had, without his really understanding why, made him feel uneasy. So uneasy, he said, that when his father had asked why he was so quiet, he hadn't known what to answer.

He fell silent.

A long time passed without his saying anything more.

She waited.

"Before dinner," he then continued – at the same moment as he got up and began to wander back and forth between the window and the foot of her bed, "before dinner I set off down to the village to buy some cigarettes, and just as I was returning home it began to rain".

They had therefore eaten indoors, he said. The atmosphere round the table had been oppressive. His father had muttered something about how ludicrous it was to interpret everything, even typical academic skirmishes, in political terms, his aunt had smiled her most absentminded smile and he himself had kept quiet from fear of the quarrel flaring up again.

Then? he said, hesitating in his stride. Well, then he had taken himself off down to the village for the second time that day.

But this time not to buy cigarettes.

"No," he said and at that moment started his restless wandering again, "then I went into the little inn beside the market place, you remember, the place we used to go to our first summer. I had some beer, smoked one cigarette after another and wrote something to you, a kind of letter which I still have on me but which I no longer want to read aloud – since I'm afraid that you'd misunderstand me, that you'd interpret my words as accusations, perhaps – well, perhaps because that's what they really are.

"But that isn't what I thought of saying.

"No," he continued, "what I want to tell you about is something quite different, an unexpected meeting.

"At the next table sat a man I thought I recognized. And after a while, as a matter of fact just as I'd finished this letter to you, he came over and introduced himself – it transpired that he was an old classmate of mine from the junior school, Frank Koch. I don't know if I've ever mentioned his name to you, I haven't seen him for many a year. Now he sat down opposite me and soon we were immersed in old memories. Frank wanted to know if I remembered how we used to spy on the pupils in the neighbouring girls' school or if I remembered the time when we had to stand in rows on the schoolyard, each with our allotted toothbrush, and brush our teeth in time, 'while the woman in a white coat at the front demonstrated all the different phases of toothbrushing on great big false teeth'. I shook my head, no, all that had vanished from my memory as if into thin air.

"What I remembered very well, on the other hand," he said, "but what I hadn't the heart to remind Frank of, was how, during the two years we were classmates before my brothers and I were hidden away in Burgenland, he had gained the respect of the whole class once by pointing to Majolika House on Linke Wienzeile and saying 'That's where I live' – a reverence and respect", he said, "that then changed into the greatest contempt when it emerged that he didn't live in one of the fashionable flats facing the street at all, as his gesture had implied, but in the poky, dark caretaker's flat in the lodge. We talked happily for a long time and drank quite a bit too. Frank", he said, "told me exhaustively and amusingly about his life as a radio salesman and about his two children. He asked if I was married, and when I answered in the affirmative he wondered if you, like his wife, had now been 'packed off to the in-laws for the summer'. I shook my head, filled his glass up and said something evasive about your being on a journey, perhaps he noticed my embarrassment for he suddenly asked quite a different question. 'And what're you doing with yourself these days?' he wanted to know. 'I seem to remember that you were interested in sport, in fact, didn't you even want to be a pilot?' I mentioned my work at the hospital, but only in passing, instead I heard myself embroidering my Semmelweis article – I spoke happily and at length about Klein and the revolution and about everything that happens in what appears to be happening, and finally he interrupted me in the middle of a sentence. 'What commitment!' he exclaimed and asked laughingly why I was getting so worked up. And I stopped short." He then said, "I didn't know what to answer."

He pondered.

"To tell the truth," he said, "I wonder myself why Semmelweis's fate effects me so strongly."

He now stood once more in front of the window, with his back to the ward.

"To get away from the subject," he said, "I asked how long Frank was staying in Nussdorf, and I don't know, no, I really don't know if it was with relief or disappointment that I learnt that he was leaving the village that same evening. We broke up immediately afterwards, and as we were parting outside the inn, both of us quite nicely drunk, I felt slightly troubled yet grateful for his having helped me to pass the time that evening.

"When I got back home the house was in darkness.

"I went to bed immediately", he said, "but I had difficulty getting off to sleep. It was only in the small hours that I fell into a light slumber, I dreamt about a rusty iron bridge and awoke with the image of a moss-covered handrail which was branded on my retina."

Here he turned quickly from the window and came over and sat down on the edge of her bed.

He took her hand.

"An apparently completely meaningless image," he said whilst stroking her fingers, "but all the same an image which made me strangely disturbed".

Then he bent forward and kissed her forehead.

The next time he came he again had flowers with him, roses now, white and only half-opened.

He laid them in front of her.

Then he stood for a while and observed her in silence before going over and sitting down by the window.

"Yesterday, early in the morning, I took a walk up towards Kahlenbergerdorf," he began.

She felt a spurt of anticipation.

"It was only a little after seven when I set off," he continued – and it was, she noticed to her amazement, as if at that moment, without even slightly brushing against her, he had taken hold of her hand, "the sun was still low and the air was fresh and easy to breathe. I walked through the sleeping village," he said. "I passed the inn, the fire-station and the churchyard on the outskirts of the village, and just as I moved on to the path that runs up between the vineyards I could smell the scent of hawthorn blossom and it struck me that I had already spent a whole week in Nussdorf.

"A whole week..." he repeated.

And now she thought it was as if they had entered a silent agreement, a kind of secret pact, in fact it was really, she thought, as if for a short time she could accompany him, out into the shimmering air – the light.

Or, he said, perhaps he ought to say endured. The atmosphere in the house was not only heavy, it was positively oppressive. He and his father worked together in the garden for short periods, well, he had already mentioned that, but they never talked about anything other than what they were busy with: the ripeness of the grapes, the distribution of the fast-growing cabbages, the insect damage to the roses. Not even during mealtimes, he said, did they discuss anything essential.

Anyway – discuss?

No, what they did was to comment on the weather, the grape harvest, or some piece of music or other they had just heard on the radio or the headlines in the day's newspaper.

And the things they never touched upon?

Well, at first he and his father avoided anything that could lead to a quarrel. Which meant that they didn't talk about von Karajan, nor about his Semmelweis article, nor about his work, about the school where his father was headmaster and least of all about the conditions at school during the actual war years. Father and aunt for their part went out of their way to avoid talking about her, he said apologetically. They no longer ever mentioned his visits to Steinhof, and if he himself said anything, which he had more or less stopped doing, they just sighed and smiled regretfully. And all three of them, Father and Aunt as well as himself, did everything in their power, yes, truly everything, he said, to avoid Uncle Karl's name.

He didn't really understand it.

There was nothing strange about he and his father wanting to avoid a quarrel, or that his father and aunt didn't know what their attitude should be towards her and the illness which wasn't really an illness – well, strictly speaking that wasn't so strange either..

But Uncle Karl?

It was incomprehensible to him that they couldn't even talk about Uncle Karl, he said. After all it was a fact that quite recently, in the period just after his death, they had talked about nothing else. At that time they had only to meet to start immediately bringing to mind different episodes from Uncle's life, they had related matters to each other that the others didn't know about – and they had laughed, he said, indeed they had actually laughed just as much as they had cried.

But now?

In some way, he said, it seemed that everything that could be said had already been said, and the only thing remaining was actually the empty place at the end of the table and a silence which grew more painful every day. Well, incidentally that was why he had already fled the house early in the morning. He had needed to be in peace, he had needed to escape making conversation at least at breakfast. And, he continued, it really was beautiful out of doors so early, quiet and peaceful, it was lovely to be able to breathe properly, and also to exert oneself too, really – the path up towards Kahlenbergerdorf was not just steep, it was also full of sharp stones and prickly, dried vegetation. Not a breeze stirred either and the only sound to be heard was the slight rustle of dry grass and gravel crunching under his shoes.

"I'd taken Céline's book on Semmelweis with me", he said, "the book that Dr Lesky, did I mention that? stuck into my hand just before I was about to leave Josephinum. 'And yet you didn't know,' she had said almost in so many words, as if in passing but all the same in a slightly triumphant tone of voice, 'you didn't know that Céline's medical thesis deals with Semmelweis.' In any case I popped this book into my pocket, and when after about an hour's wandering I found an empty bench – at that point I had not only passed Kahlenbergerdorf but also gone a further kilometre or so up through the forest I sank down on it, tired and contented to read.

"You should have seen the place, by the way," he said, "what a view you had, with the town glistening in hazy sunlight far below and with the blue mountains to the south-east."

He fell silent.

Then he came over to her. "How thoughtless of me," he murmured, and bent down for the roses. He disappeared but returned after a while with a vase which he placed on the small table by her bedhead. Then he returned to his place by the window.

She waited.

Gradually he took up his narrative again. At first the words came slowly and tentatively, but after only a short while he was up to his usual fast and rather definite tempo.

How much time had passed while he sat there on the bench, he said, he really didn't know.

Perhaps two hours, perhaps even three.

The sun had climbed ever higher in the sky and it had slowly grown warmer.

"I tried to read," he said, "but I had difficulty in concentrating. Thoughts were buzzing around in my head. I was forced to read the same passage again and again, and although Céline's view of Semmelweis really interested me I only managed to get through about twenty pages. Yes, the fact is", he said, "that the only thing I really remember of what I read is something from the preface, which wasn't even Céline's own, a few lines about the striking similarities between Céline's and Semmelweis's personalities and the 'moving' fact – 'moving' according to the author of the preface considering Céline's fierce anti-Semitism – that Semmelweis was a Jew.

"Magda", he said, "can you imagine that the girl in the bookshop was right after all! It's remarkable, especially since I've not come across the information about Semmelweis's Jewish extraction anywhere else!"

He gave a laugh.

Well, he said, afterwards, when after the tiring walk downhill he had finally reached Nussdorf, he had had a headache, it was surely at least thirty degrees, and in order to cool down and to slake his thirst, perhaps also to postpone his return home, he had sat for half-an-hour or so at the inn where he had had a beer and written down a few of the thoughts that had so persistently disturbed him in his reading. When he had got back to the house his aunt had just laid lunch in the garden, and for the first time, he said, it had been almost a relief to hear her chatter – about some new murdered woman and about the total incompetence of the Viennese police who still hadn't succeeded in arresting little Dagmar's murderer.

"Magda…!" he said.

And now suddenly he was standing right up to her again. He sat down on the edge of the bed and bent over her; when he continued to speak she could feel the moist warmth of his breath.

192

Smoke, passed through her mind. Incense…

"Magda," he whispered, "what really happened?

"What did I do wrong?

"I only wanted to spare you from remembering," he said, "I wanted you to be happy."

She waited.

What a peculiar smell, she thought, sweet and almost nauseating.

"Some time ago," he continued, "I don't know if you remember it – some time ago you told me about the district in Budapest where you grew up. I remember that you described a huge chestnut tree which you climbed up into as a child, and I remember that you then talked at length and in detail about the room you shared with your mother. It was so strange to hear you describe all that, you became so – different.

"I think," he said in a hesitant voice, "I think that at that moment, although I didn't want to admit it even to myself, I realized that I was on the point of losing you.

"And the boy?

"What part, this question too I have often asked myself, what part has that József played in what's happened- who was he really?

"Magda," he wondered, "that little Jószef – who was he really?"

Soon after that he squeezed her hand hard, got up from the bed and left the ward.

The next time he came he went straight over and sat down in the window.

"Magda," he said and she had a feeling that while he was speaking he was trying incessantly to catch her eye, "I've now finished Céline's book on Semmelweis, that medical thesis I was telling you about the other day. I've…" he said – but at that moment he got stuck.

Although now, he then continued almost in the same breath, now that he yet again, as so often during his earlier visits, heard himself mention Semmelweis's name – well, then suddenly he didn't really know why he did so.

He really couldn't understand, he said, why Semmelweis's fate disturbed him so profoundly.

And even less, he said, why he persisted in telling her about it.

And so extensively, and in the most minute detail.

"Nevertheless," he said, and she noticed now that he had finally stopped observing her, that indeed he sat with his forehead resting against the windowpane – as if his gaze was searching for something out there, "nevertheless I can't stop".

Sometimes, he continued, sometimes he told himself that it depended on just that. What he had mentioned earlier. That there were certain points of contact.

He halted for a moment.

"Certain points of contact…" he murmured and stuck out a hand in a broad gesture which seemed to encompass not only the nearest park out there but the whole area, far beyond Baum-gartnerhöhe.

But more often, he added, much more often he thought that it was mostly to – well, to be spared from…

Then suddenly he changed direction again.

"Magda," he said and straightened up with a jerk. "Céline's book was much more interesting than I had expected! You see, Céline", he continued quickly, "Céline hardly mentions the political power game – for him it's the artist who stands in the centre". Like all geniuses, he said, Semmelweis, according to Céline, was too great for his times, his genius was, a strange thought, even too great for himself: it consumed him, tore him apart from within – in fact, he said, according to Céline it was ultimately Semmelweis's creative genius that brought about his downfall. And instead of emphasizing the revolutions that were taking place everywhere in society, not least in the universities

194

Céline laid great stress on what he called Semmelweis's madness – she should just see, he said, in what strong colours and with what powerful strokes Céline painted the picture of a Semmelweis who, misunderstood by everyone, searched for secrets in the walls, who laughed without reason and who talked to himself about signs, persecutions and heavenly bodies.

"Heavenly bodies!" he exclaimed. "Good heavens, Magda, that's just something Céline made up!"

He laughed quietly to himself.

"You can't imagine," he said. "Oh, it's so interesting.

"Céline fantasises, he blends fact and fiction as it suits him.

"Perhaps not even consciously.

"And", he further explained, "what doesn't tally with the picture of Semmelweis, the solitary, magnificent and self-destroying genius – he quite simply ignores. The fact that Semmelweis worked virtually up until his death, that after his return to Budapest he married and that he had two children whom he loved more than anything else in the world – well, such small bagatelles Céline quite simply omits to mention.

"This was something I hadn't expected.

"No," he said – and now all at once he sounded pensive, "I must say that Céline's interpretation surprised me."

He was silent for a while.

"Magda?" he then asked, "are we really so governed by the thought patterns that surround us?

"Is our interpretation of reality so little objective and to such a high degree a result not only of our own times but of our own personality?

"I must admit," he said finally, "I must admit that thought also scares me slightly."

"Just listen to this!" he cried a few days later.

"I've checked up on the matter – Semmelweis in fact wasn't a Jew at all!

"Do you see?" he laughed.

"For Dr Lesky, now at the beginning of the Sixties, Semmelweis was a victim of political intrigue. For the aspiring writer
Céline he was a victim of creation, of the self-consuming power
of genius.

"And during the war – well, the Nazis quite simply made him
a Jew.

"Why? one may ask oneself. Did the Nazis want to stress
their own scientific achievements by belittling Semmelweis?

"Yes, I suppose that's it.

"If it really was the Nazis themselves who gave him that new
affiliation. And not the resistance movement. Which in itself",
he said, "bearing in mind that such a movement scarcely existed
in our country, is hardly likely. But even so. Semmelweis was the
perfect victim – in every sense.

"Dear God, Magda, how is all this possible?"

"And what about me?" he wanted to know.

He had just arrived. Had sat for a while on the edge of her
bed without saying anything, had played with her fingers,
stroked her cheek, smoothed the pillow under her head. Then
he had murmured something about the heat, about the town
down there being like a boiling cauldron and about the streets
lying covered in a fine, yellow dust. "It will thunder by this
evening," he had added before getting up and going over to the
window.

"And what about me?" he asked again. "What are the invisible screens through which I observe the world around me?"

He leant forward against the window.

"You know," he said, "just now I notice with horror that in
spite of everything, I have a certain sympathy for – the conservative Professor Klein. Or perhaps not so much for Klein as for
those who found themselves a little further from the centre of
events, Semmelweis's colleagues elsewhere."

He cleared his throat, slightly troubled.

He couldn't help it, he said. But all the same, one must in the name of justice look at all the theories prevalent at the time. And she couldn't imagine, he said, all the things one blamed for puerperal fever. Heavens, they talked about everything from epidemics to such things as the consequences of a difficult delivery, mental instability in the form of anxiety, depression, guilt, an unconscious desire to be rid of the child or sheer fear of death, they talked about draughts and bad air, of milk stoppage, diarrhoea, too quick a delivery of the placenta, the wrong diet or corsets that were too tight – in fact, he said, generally speaking, the only thing they were all agreed on was that the causes were numerous.

He laughed.

In any case, he said, if one saw the matter from the perspective of the period Semmelweis's stubborn assertion that there was one, and only one, cause must have seemed insane, to put it mildly. Semmelweis talked about corpse poison, he said, but there were demonstrably masses of cases where post-mortems hadn't occurred. And therefore, he said, therefore it wasn't strange that one, according to good scientific custom, as it were, refused to throw all previous knowledge overboard in preference for something that one didn't really know what it was.

Here he sank suddenly into silence.

It was only after a long while that he began to speak again.

"Magda, he then said, "am I quite simply afraid?

"Do I have a latent desire to smooth over, in fact to a certain extent excuse such things as stupidity, rigidity, narrow-mindedness and lust for power?

"Afraid?

"And therefore cowardly too?"

He stopped and made as if to leave his place at the window – but then looked back out towards the park again. "All day yesterday," he said, " the whole day I was full of such reflections.

In the evening I had difficulty in getting to sleep. It wasn't until I'd smoked at least half a packet of cigarettes and drunk masses of Aunt's sweet, white wine that I fell asleep.

"And then," he said, "I had a hideous dream. A dream which was partly like many of my earlier ones – have I told you by the way that I was already starting to dream about houses when I was young? But this dream – well, it was worse than any of the others.

"I came home to a house," he said, "very similar to the one my brothers and I lived in during the war, now yours and mine. The house was in a better condition than I'd expected, it pleased me – and yet I soon realized that there was something wrong. After a short search I found a carton which shouldn't have been there. I opened it, carefully and with a pounding heart – and discovered to my horror that it contained two sev-ered feet. And when at that same moment I noticed that my hands were sticky with the stinking, light rose-coloured fleshy juice that was seeping out through the bottom of the carton. I experienced a feeling of disgust so strong that I woke up."

He paused for a short while.

"Still feeling rather nauseous." he concluded, "I got up and went out into the garden to get some fresh air. I sat for a long time on the garden sofa looking out over the dark valley. Only when the first signs of dawn appeared did I go back in."

"Yesterday morning," he said, "Father and I worked for an hour or so in the garden. We were just spraying the dark red Hadley roses with soapy water when Martin suddenly turned up from out of the greenery.

"Father's face lit up," he said.

Then he stopped.

She waited, impatient now.

"It was Thursday of course," he continued, "but Martin, it transpired, had unexpectedly been given time off from the editorial office. Elise and the children were also there. Whilst

Martin miopically inspected a leaf speckled black with aphid he murmured something about their helping to lay the table. Whereupon, he said, after having communicated this fact, Martin had walked round for a long time admiring the roses; the salmon pink and yellow ones had particularly aroused his delight. On the way back to the house Martin had then asked how his Semmelweis article was coming on. He'd then explained that he'd already written part of it, but that he'd probably need a few more weeks to complete it. At that Martin had laughed and declared that he hadn't asked in order to hurry him up, he was merely interested. What's more, he said, Martin had said that he was convinced the article would be fine. "I know", he had said, "that you have the right attitude".

"The right attitude?" he said, "Has Martin any idea what attitude I have to things?"

In the garden, he continued, they had met Aunt. The meal would soon be ready. "I washed my hands in the kitchen," he said, "and then went up to my room to change. While I was looking for a clean shirt I listened to the radio. They were interviewing somebody, the whole thing seemed to deal with a very prominent leader of the police at that time who must have had something to do with the arrest of Anne Frank. They talked about revenge, about justice and about the danger of collective guilt. And then I heard something that brought me up with a start, indeed that made me stand there for a long time with the shirt half over my head: 'Masses of people' the interviewee more or less said, 'maintain today that during the war they had saved several Jews from annihilation. But that is a downright lie. For if it were true Austria would have had twice as big a Jewish population after the war as before.

"A downright lie? I thought, horrified.

"And Uncle Karl?'

"'You've left two shirt buttons undone', Elise pointed out when I sat down at the table in the garden. Aunt carved the joint

of ham, Martin passed round the dish with knödel. Father asked
Martin if he was pleased with his mandolin. The flies buzzed;
it was warm even in the shade. I asked Martin if he remembered
Frank Koch. Martin thought about it. 'Frank Koch,' he then
wondered, wasn't he that scrawny, red-haired lad who lived in
Majolika house?' I told him that I'd met Frank here in Nussdorf
a while ago and that he was a radio salesman nowadays. That
we'd sat discussing childhood memories half the night. 'Have a
little more sauerkraut', Aunt said. Erich whined that he wanted
to go bathing. 'On Sunday,' Martin said curtly. Elisabeth took
Erich with her over to the hammock.

"I hesitated," he said. "After which I made up my mind and
accounted in detail for what I had just heard on the radio.
'"Twice as many,' I said, 'just imagine, twice as many after the
war as before.'" Here he was silent for a moment.

It had gone very silent round the table, he then said. Nobody
had said a word about what they were all thinking. An eternity
passed. Then the Aunt got up to clear the table. Nonsense,
Father had muttered and got up too. Elise had followed them
into the house. Martin and he had remained alone at the table.

Martin, he said, had squirmed in embarrassment.

And after a while Martin had asked if he would like to go with
him to Donau Insel to do some fishing on Sunday.

He'd told him he'd go if he had time.

After that he was silent again.

"Magda," he asked at last, "Have I ever told you that my
mother was half-Jewish?"

Yesterday evening, he said, he had been up in Canovagasse.

He had been there because his father had asked him to collect
the post.

The flat had been hot and dusty, he said, it smelt stuffy. He
had been seized by a slight nausea and had hurried to open the
windows, then he had gone out on to the balcony to have a

smoke. He had lit a cigarette, had a few drags and leant against the wall. The street down below lay deserted, the sky over Karlskirche was dark blue. He had let his eye wander slowly from the church and the park to the house opposite theirs, out of the corner of his eye he had seen the living-room's other balcony and he had thought that the distance was greater than he remembered it, at least three metres, perhaps four. That was Martin's balcony, he had also thought, this one was his own. Martin's was at one time an Atlantic cruiser, the next time a helicopter. His, on the other hand, was a Zeppelin, always the same.

"And then, quite unexpectedly," he said, "I also remembered something else, I remembered how we used to interrupt our game, how we used to climb up on to the rung second from the top of our balustrade, stick our feet under the black iron leaves, rest our knees against the top and lean over with the intention of trying to reach each other's fingertips, just as far out as we could. Yes, Martin and I really did stretch out towards each other over the abyss – without, it now seems, reflecting for a moment on how easy it would have been to slip, to lose our balance (the slightest change in the centre of gravity would have been devastating) or that a fall could have crushed our skulls like eggshells against the pavement's stone slabs.

"I remember," he said hesitantly, "I remember as well how much I'd loved those moments and that I was in fact always the first to urge them on."

Then he fell silent.

After a while she had the impression that he was crying.

"Magda," he whispered at last, "what is it that's happening?"

"Magda…?"

He cleared his throat. Then he mentioned something about having almost missed the buss out to Nussdorf and that he had had difficulty in getting to sleep as usual.

He had not been able to forget the image of the two balconies, he explained. Of the balconies or of the great distance between them. And just as he was drifting off to sleep he had suddenly, with painful clarity, seen Martin's small figure on the top of the black balustrade. For a lightning moment he had been able to feel the warmth from the sunlit wall, the coldness of the iron against his knees and – like a violent intake of breath – the light, tickling excitement changed into pure terror: before his eyes and without being able to do anything to prevent it, Martin had lost his grip of the rail and fallen headlong towards the pavement down below.

Wide awake once more he had got up.

And since he had then been far too upset even to think of sleep he had sat down at the desk and started to work on his Semmelweis article.

"I didn't go and lie down again," he said, "until it grew light".

"I did go to Donau Insel."

He bent over and stroked her cheek.

"Magda"...? he whispered.

Then he got up and went over to the window.

"We cycled along the river," he said, "Martin with Erich on the luggage carrier, Elise, Elisbeth and I.

"Northwards from Reichsbrücke."

"The banks were full of people fishing, out on the water a host of white sails glistened. The crickets were singing. Near Jedleseer Brücke we met a very old man in a black cap, with a walking stick in one hand and a naked little boy on the other. The boy laughed and waved when he caught sight of us. After half-an-hour or so we found a secluded spot where we stopped and laid out our packed lunch. As soon as the children had eaten they ran down to the water to play. Elise dozed in the sun. Martin and I sat down on some stones to fish, Erich was with us for a short time, but he soon got tired of that and went back to his sister.

"I asked Martin if he remembered our game with the balconies in Canovagasse, he laughed and said that he did. Very well. 'I also remember', he said, 'that I was rather envious of you because your balcony was a Zeppelin'.

"This surprised me: I'd never looked at the matter in that way.

"'Why didn't you ask to swap with me?' I wondered.

"He merely shrugged his shoulders.

"Then we sat in silence for a long while. I had wanted to ask him about Uncle Karl. I had wanted to know what Martin thought about what I had heard on the radio, if he too wondered whether Uncle Karl's efforts on behalf of Jews during the war was a myth, a lie in line with other lies. Yet I didn't say anything, I don't know why, perhaps I quite simply wished that he himself would broach the subject. The water glistened, for the first time as long as I can remember the river really was blue. And suddenly, to my own surprise, I heard myself pose a quite different question: 'Martin,' I said. 'Can you tell me why Mother really drowned?'

"'Yes,' he then said, 'Really the question caught not least myself unawares.

"And yet," he added, "at the very moment I heard myself utter the forbidden words I also knew why I'd done so: one could just as well have lied to us about Mother as about Uncle Karl. And wasn't it in fact strange that Mother, who was not only a good swimmer but also a very cautious person had decided so late one autumn evening to swim right across the lake – a distance of several kilometres. Well, one can't help wondering whether her drowning was the result not of imprudence but of free will – but then what reason could she have had? This is just what more and more frequently I have started to ask myself: what reasons could there have been? And then I have to wonder about Father. Father's position as headmaster during the war was very sensitive and perhaps, it isn't at any rate impossible, perhaps Mother was afraid that she, half-Jewish, would be a burden to him – indeed perhaps at the time of the tragic event Mother had really begun to consider herself an encumbrance. And in that case – did Father understand that? Had they discussed the matter? In short – could Father have done anything to prevent what happened?

"Now I said nothing about all this. I merely asked that one question: Did Martin know why Mother had drowned?

"Naturally Martin got upset and deeply troubled; nor had I expected anything else. At first he looked at me, hurt, then he turned away.

"I fell silent, seized by a slight giddiness. It felt as though everything around me was on the point of slipping out of my hands, as if I was on the point of completely losing my grip on existence. I didn't know what to do or how to continue. For a brief moment I considered quite simply getting up and leaving. But then something occurred that I definitely hadn't expected: Martin put down his rod, clenched his fists, looked with a pensive expression out over the river and told me – that once many years ago he had asked Father about it.

"Father! I thought in confusion. It's not possible!

"Father, Martin continued, had mentioned to him something that later he would never be able to forget. According to Father, Martin said, Mother loved life, deeply and passionately – but at the same time, or perhaps just because of that, she was desperately afraid of death. In fact, according to Father, ever since childhood Mother had been completely possessed by the thought that any of her nearest and dearest or she herself could die. Every waking moment of the day, Father apparently had said, death had been present in Mother's conscious world. 'It was obvious', Martin said, 'that Father considered Mother's death to be both an accident and a case of suicide, even if a half-hearted one: to swim so far out on the lake on a cold autumn evening seemed in Father's eyes to have been a way of testing

204

the boundaries, a way of either conclusively overcoming death or finally allowing the inevitable to become a reality.'

"At Martin's words I began to tremble, it required all my strength not to burst into tears.

"And yet I felt a strange kind of relief too.

"We were silent – for an eternity it seemed to me. Finally Martin cleared his throat, it almost sounded as though he regretted what he had said. Then I did something I hadn't done since we were young teenagers: I bent down and ruffled his hair. Martin's face lit up and he looked at me with an expression so full of gratitude that I felt ashamed."

He was silent.

When soon afterwards he left the ward she had the greatest desire to call him back.

The next day he was very upset.

"I've left Nussdorf for good," he exclaimed before he had even had time to reach her bed. For a brief moment he looked irresolute, then he began to walk with long strides back and forth between the bed and the window.

Yesterday evening, he explained, he and his father had got into such a violent and disturbing quarrel that he had immediately gathered his things together and left. Oh, he said, if he only knew how to describe to her what had happened. "If", he said "I could at least understand how the whole thing started".

Then he halted in the middle of a stride and instead sat down by the foot of her bed.

He had come down from his room after having sat for an hour or so working on his article, he said, and now the words suddenly poured out of him: his father had been on an errand in the village, they had bumped into each other on the outdoor steps, and when his father had suggested that they should sit together in the garden for a while he had agreed immediately, it was such a beautiful evening, the air was fresh after the thunder that morning, there was the scent of roses, it was calm. They each sat in an easy chair, he lit a cigarette, his father asked if he had begun to feel rested, if it was nice not to be working at the clinic. They chatted a little about this and that, the aunt came out and sat with them for a while, then the telephone rang and she disappeared back inside. Then he couldn't remember what had happened – suddenly the quarrel was quite simply in full swing. Somehow, he said, von Karajan's name came up – afterwards he could imagine it had happened automatically, almost as if language was autonomous, as if it lived its own life quite beyond their will: suddenly he simply heard himself in the most indignant terms lecture about something von Karajan was recently guilty of – as if, he now said, I should bother so much about von Karajan's ridiculous initiatives! – it was something about von Karajan in the middle of a rehearsal having turned to one of his oldest friends and collaborators, looked at him and remarked that the latter had brown eyes, imagine, von Karajan was supposed to have said in a chilling tone, traitor's eyes. He had, he said, heard himself shout something about this man who considered himself the instrument of God on earth, and he had heard himself demand that his father answer: did his father defend such a remark or not, whereupon, he said, his father instead answered something completely different, something to do with von Karajan's production of *Boris Godunov*, which in turn, he said, annoyed him himself even further, since he had seen it as a way of avoiding the question – although afterwards he wondered if it really was.

"Anyway," he said, "we started again, for the umpteenth time, to squabble about von Karajan's membership of the Nazi party. As usual Father defended him and contended that that was von Karajan's sacrifice on the altar of music and that it had been a terrible decision for him to make – something von Karajan himself had ludicrously denied, which naturally I immediately pointed out, doubtless in quite vehemently – in fact I wonder if Father didn't touch on the thought that only someone lacking a conscience can be a true genius. I myself objected, even more vehemently, that Father was quite mistaken and that von Karajan had actually joined the party twice – the second time perhaps forced into it for tactical, let's call it artistic, reasons, but the first time, on the other hand, from his own convictions. 'Don't shout!' said Father. 'And anyway you've said yourself that you admire his work with the Berlin Philharmonic.' I objected that that had nothing to do with the matter, but Father shrugged his shoulders and then, he said, at least I think that's what happened, then he said that I ought to reflect that in the middle of the war von Karajan had married someone half-Jewish.

"And, Father explained and looked at me with a most reproving gaze, even you must surely admit what a brave action that was!"

Then, he said, well, then he had suddenly been filled with such fury that he almost fainted. Without a word he had got up, left the room, packed his things and vacated the house, by the back way so as not to meet Father who presumably was still sitting out in the garden.

"In the garden…" he said and stopped.

"Now I'm sleeping in my room at the hospital," he added, "and I've decided two things: in what's left of my holiday I'm thinking of finding the Hungarian research worker whose name Dr Lesky gave me, he's called Sarbó, I believe – I already applied for a visa to Budapest yesterday – and when I come back in a week or so I'm thinking of looking up Father and demanding from him information about Uncle Karl, about my mother's death and about other things he's kept from me, goodness knows what he can have kept quiet about through the years. Yes, well, on my return I shall finally put to him the questions I've so far not been able to formulate, not even to myself."

Here he suddenly got up and went over to the window.

"But", he continued after a short hesitation, "there's another thing too."

Yesterday, he said, late yesterday afternoon he had been up in the flat in Hockegasse to fetch his passport – well, he had met the caretaker, incidentally, who wondered when she, Magda, was coming home, and a while later, just as he sat talking to his Australian research colleague, the caretaker's wife had come up with a jar of plum jam, and she had wondered the same thing – "because, it transpired, a little girl had been there several times asking for you. I presume it was that pupil you had last spring, now what was it she was called?"

Anyway, he said, when he afterwards was looking for his passport he had found a letter – on the piano in the living-room.

He presumed that she knew what it was he was talking about.

Some time in the spring, he said, she had obviously written that letter to József. And she had had the letter returned unopened.

"Magda", he then said, "I've thought about it all night.

"If you like, as soon as you come back home, we can try to find out the boy's address together.

"We can enquire from the Swedish authorities.

"If you like," he said, "if you like, we could perhaps even look him up – we could write to his foster parents and agree on a suitable time and place. We can surely get them to change their minds – in fact together surely we can persuade them that in spite of everything the boy needs you."

At last! He was back at last!

"It's impossible to see the town from here today," he said. "The whole valley's covered in mist. The sky's greyish white too, and the trees are dripping wet."

He leant forward against the window.

"And yet they're playing football down there again today, four patients and a carer and the referee of course, in his wheelchair."

Oh, it was such a relief to hear him talk.

Did she know incidentally, he wondered, that he'd met the poor soul on the way here, just inside the hospital gate. "He stopped me and asked for a light," he said. "When I'd lit his cigarette he giggled loudly and uncontrollably, and when I then continued past him he began to move his wheelchair round and round there on the gravel path, with the burning cigarette in the corner of his mouth the whole time and in ever-diminishing circles until finally he toppled over and I had to rush back and help him up. And do you know what happened then? Well, the poor skinny lad flung his arms around my neck, looked me deep in the eyes and asked if I was a photographer, because if I wasn't, he explained, then I had a double in a photographer's shop in the first district. 'In the shop in Sterngasse', he then shouted after me, 'in that dark little hovel where my dad works!

"It's..." he said pensively.

Then he got stuck.

She waited impatiently.

His visa had disappeared, he said after a while. It had taken three weeks for the embassy to arrange the whole thing so that he could finally leave Budapest. It was already 29 August today, more than a month, that is, since he was last here.

He cleared his throat.

It was remarkable, he then said. The trees were still green, the lawn down below was full of yellow flowers, and even if the sky was covered in mist it was very warm – and yet there was an unmistakable feeling of autumn in the air.

Yes, it was obvious that something had changed.

But what?

"Is it only our expectations?" he wondered. "Is it only the knowledge about nature's fluctuations that makes us see everything with different eyes?"

He hesitated slightly.

But, he then continued, she would naturally be wondering about his impressions of Hungary.

The only thing was, he said, that he hardly knew what to say. She knew about everything so much better than he did, after all.

Besides which, he said, he'd spent most of his time running around between the embassy and different authorities, except of course, he added, the evenings which he had spent at different gloomy restaurants where he had eaten his way through every imaginable variation of goulash, stuffed cabbage and an insipid, grey mass which they insisted on calling chestnut purée, drunk beer and flicked through his notes – he had met that fellow Sarbó, which really was his name, several times the first week, and since he'd had a great deal to say about Semmelweis, there had also been a lot of material to go through.

He laughed suddenly.

"He, Sarbó, that is," he said, and now all at once he sounded almost eager, " was a strange man, you know, a real bruiser, big, a neck like a bull, a wrestler type, but with an unusually lively temperament. On the first day he insisted on showing me the house where Semmelweis was born, it lay high up on the Buda side and presented a sorry sight, bombed to bits and dilapidated as it was, but whilst Dr Sarbó – he's a psychiatrist, incidentally, not an immunologist or medical historian – whilst he led me up to a café near the castle he swore that it was to be restored, in fact within the course of a few years it would have been trans-formed into a monument worthy of his great countryman.

"My great countryman", he said, "that's what Sarbó said the whole time during our walk, and in fact later too during our hours-long conversations when, coughing and chain-smoking he showered me with proof that Semmelweis in fact had been insane: 'Semmelweis', he came back to it again and again, 'Ignaz Philipp Semmelweis was presumably already infected in his youth by something, probably syphilis, and suffered ever since then from latent paralysis. From *dementia paralytica*', he hissed and stared at me with his burning eyes, 'and it was just that, that insidious mental illness that was the true cause of his misfortunes.'

"Good heavens, Magda, it was impossible to get Dr Sarbó to stop.

"Sarbó", he said, "positively showered me with what he called 'proof' of Semmelweis's illness. He brought up Semmelweis's 'unnatural' irritability, his often very 'sharp' tone of voice and his 'stereotypical' repetition of one and the same argument – as if anybody in Semmelweis's desperate situation wouldn't have reacted exactly like him.

"What's more," he said, "Sarbó maintained that Semmelweis suffered from pathological fixations, from an inability to take a broad view, from morbid verbosity and persecution mania – good heavens! He pointed out that Semmelweis had often appeared unstable and even sexually provocative, which naturally he was unable to give any examples of, and finally he concluded his discourse by declaring quite openly that Semmelweis, not just for his own good but for the good of those around him, ought to have been taken in charge at a very early stage.

"I must say," he said, "that Sarbó's comments shocked me, at least at first; gradually I grew more and more fascinated, and the more Sarbó with his frenetic zeal embroidered on Semmelweis's character – 'spiritual decadence' incidentally was a continually repeated phrase, as was 'patient', well, one really got a feeling that everybody according to Sarbó's personal philosophy was a latent patient – indeed, the more Sarbó went on talking, the clearer I realized that the muscular, chain-smoking wrestler on the opposite side of the café table wasn't really talking about Semmelweis's era at all but about his own, and that the whole of his research work was one long justification for the right of the Soviet power to place people with divergent and uncomfortable opinions in safe custody in a mental hospital."

He paused for a little while.

"Yes," he said musingly, that was exactly how he had perceived it. "Yes," he said," it was, I must say, with a growing feeling of distaste that I listened to this Hungarian colleague. His conversation appalled me since it made me realize still more clearly how governed we all are, in scientific work too, by our surroundings and the patterns of thought in which we work.

"His words appalled me.

"But", he went on, "they frightened me too – they filled me with an insidious, horrid perception which then, when I had lost my visa and was met everywhere by the same chilling suspicion, grew increasingly strong every day".

Yes, he said, it had been a relief, in every way a relief, when finally he had been able to leave Budapest.

She waited.

After a while he came and sat down beside her.

"Magda," he then said, "why does it have to be so difficult…have to be so difficult to. … to remain questioning, not to be content with having understood once and for all?"

To have understood, he said – and now he took her hand.

They had talked about it of course, he said. The expression "I understand". But wasn't that in fact something of a paradox?

"Now," he said tentatively, "now all the same I think that perhaps it implies not only ossification but also – movement. Well, couldn't it, at the same time as embracing a need for control, for a strong longing for a final, once-and-for-all accepted truth, for order, stability, calm – 'I understand' as a kind of incantation of death's darkness – could it not at the same time imply the opposite: an equally strong longing to penetrate more deeply, a willingness to listen and, in fact, to increase one's knowledge?"

He fell silent.

Then he bent over her hand and kissed it – before getting up and hurrying back to his place at the window.

"The clouds have started to break up," he said after a while. "It looks as if it's going to be a lovely evening."

Then he laid his head against the window frame. And what else? he continued in a hesitant voice, what else had he done in Budapest, as well as listening to Sarbó and waiting for a new visa?

Well, he said, he had drunk masses of beer, but he had already mentioned that, and then he had listened to one zigeuner orchestra after another – God, he said, how tired he had been of that melancholy music! – and sometimes, in the mornings, he had sat in the park beside the hotel and watched the old men playing chess.

One day, he said, he had made an excursion by paddle-steamer on the Danube. It was a hot day and lovely with a cooling breeze from the water.

Then he had gone bathing, of course, at outdoor baths on Margaret Island. He had also got into conversation with an elderly man there, an old war veteran – one of his legs had been amputated. They had talked mostly about music, but also about other things, and when he had asked the old man what he thought about what had happened in Fifty-six he had waved away the question, just as Sarbó had done, incidentally, with the explanation that he had forgotten everything from that time. So much has changed since then, the old man had answered to his own surprise.

He was, he said, a very sympathetic man.

When he himself had mentioned that his wife was from Hungary the old man had beamed with happiness, embraced him and kissed him on both cheeks.

He laughed slightly: "Well," he said," then I walked around a great deal of course – but here he suddenly stopped.

He hesitated.

"Yes, well," he said, "one evening...

"...one evening I actually found my way to Szigony utca, to the house where you grew up.

"And there," he said slowly, "well, everything was just as you had described it.

"In the courtyard grew a large chestnut tree," he said, "and the ground underneath was covered with conkers which the children were playing with...

"Round a table a few old men were sitting, playing chess.

"Outside the windows there was washing hanging out to dry.

"And music was pouring out from a radio on the second floor.

"Liszt," he said. "Scherzo and March."

Then he fell silent.

After a while he began to pace back and forth in front of the window.

"Magda..." he said and held back for a moment.

Then he resumed his pacing again.

Back – and forth. Back – and forth.

"Although sometimes," he murmured, mostly it seemed to have something to say, "well, sometimes when I felt too lonely, then I went to the Austrian Embassy and read the newspapers".

At that there followed a long pause.

"Read the newspapers..." he murmured.

Then he stopped short again.

"By the way," he said and now his voice had suddenly regained something of its energetic tone, "by the way, I almost forgot: I saw in today's paper this morning on the way to the hospital, in today's *Neuer Kurier* there's a long article on the Opera murderer – the police have finally arrested the man who stabbed Dagmar Fuhrich to death at the beginning of the year.

"Do you remember? he said. "The little ballet pupil"

He leant against the window frame.

"The murderer", he said, "is called Josef Weinwurm, he's thirty-two and was already known to the police: as a sixteen-year-old he'd already threatened a girl with a pistol, because, so it says in the paper, he wanted to see her naked, and in later years he's apparently specialized in robbing people, especially in queues at theatres, cinemas, and, not least, the Opera. You can imagine", he said, "how Aunt is going to react.

"My goodness, yes", he added, "it will be her only topic of conversation for the next few weeks – and not only her, incidentally. This is something that will occupy the whole of Vienna for a long time to come."

He rubbed his hand over his eyes.

But when you think about it, he said. Was that really something to be surprised about?

"Aunt", he then said, "is always talking about murders, as you know – about the latest sex murder. She talks with emotional insight about the victims, she laments their fate and she's horrified at the suffering they must have endured – but mostly, yes," he said, "above all, it strikes me now, in fact more than anything else she's interested in the murderer.

"In the perpetrator of the crime."

His aunt, he said pensively, would admittedly spend hours scrutinizing the execution of the deed, she would immerse herself in details around the actual method, around such things as waylaying, stabbing, traces of blood and escape routes – but her most profound commitment, all the questions she continually came back to, always touched upon the same thing: the murderer's motive, his state of mind and the degree of guilt.

His aunt, he said, always wanted to know what sort of upbringing the murderer had had, and if when the crime had been committed he had been in full possession of his senses. And if that were not the case, he said, if the deed had been committed in a fit of confusion and if the murderer when he had cast himself over the victim had been driven by a desire stronger than himself – well, then she wanted to know to what extent in such circumstances he could be considered responsible for his actions, that's to say, he said, his aunt wanted in that case to question his guilt.

One could, he said, and presumably this was how his aunt reasoned, one could naturally consider a murderer to be mad – but that put him into a different category from the one that applied to ordinary people – his crime then assumed a different, perhaps less threatening, character. If the perpetrator was accountable on the other hand then it immediately became a different matter. Then, he said, one had to decide whether he was a more evil person than others or if everybody in his situation would have acted exactly as he had.

His aunt, he continued hesitantly, loved to draw parallels, as she no doubt recalled, between present-day sexual murderers and Musil's famous Moosbrugger. "But what is it that she's really doing, then?"

In Musil's novel, he said, as far as he could remember, a penetrating discussion had been carried on about Moosbrugger's character, about his possible insanity and about his equally possible culpability – about his guilt, as it were. And now when he came to think about it, it was naturally no coincidence that his aunt looked for her references in Musil – the period that Musil captured so well, it occurred to him now, was not only the time of their own childhood, but just as much Aunt's period, in fact if Ulrich, he said, if the man without properties had been living today, which for that matter perhaps he did, then Aunt and he would be practically speaking contemporaries.

"An amusing thought!"

He gave a short laugh.

"Be that as it may", he continued, "I remember that Musil somewhere in his novel maintains that if humanity could dream, it would conjure up a sex murderer just like Moosbrugger – and it's exactly the same in our age, of course. To think that I didn't realize it before!"

He laughed again.

"Oh," he said, "little Dagmar Fuhrich's murderer, that despicable Josef Weinwurm, is quite simply our nightmares' answer to the experiences of our times – he has, one might say, sprung forth from our memories of the war, Nazism and the persecutions, from a feeling of implication, guilt, inadequacy, impotence and fury." He pressed his fingertips together. "Dear God," he said, "when Aunt talks about the Opera murderer, she's actually speaking from an extremely personal trauma. Talking about Josef Weinwurm becomes, for each and every one of us, a way of tackling our fear of the evil aspects of ourselves. Yes, good heavens, Magda, I can see it so clearly now: we keep silent about the past by continually talking about it – but in a disguised form. And perhaps in fact, just like Musil's loveable Clarissa, we all dream of saving the murderer by our own good- ness not of saving Josef Weinwurm of course, but the sinful aspect of own selves.

"Perhaps," he said, "that's just it".

It also occurred to him now that Clarissa had had another preposterous idea. Clarissa, he said, considered, quite without reason, that Moosbrugger was musical.

"A musical genius."

Naturally, he said, naturally that had nothing, no, truly absolutely nothing to do with von Karajan – "but neverthe- less, it was that business about musicality that made me think about him, or about Father's and my quarrels about his character."

Yes, he said, didn't von Karajan perform the same function for his father and him as Moosbrugger for his aunt – when his father and he quarrelled about von Karajan their quarrel was really about something quite different, something much more dangerous, something that they didn't dare call by its true name.

"When Father and I quarrel about von Karajan", he said, "and as you know, our quarrels really aren't about his interpre- tations of musical works but about his personal attitudes – well, then we're really having a conversation about something which, if we were to dare talk about it openly, would sweep us up into a tornado of hatred."

Of hatred, he said. A hatred which, at least that was no doubt what they both feared, could perhaps crush them.

He then leant his head against the wall behind him and was lost in thought.

A long time passed – so long that she was afraid that he had finished speaking.

"Yesterday," he then began once more, "I actually met Father yesterday, by chance."

Did she remember, he wondered, did she remember that before he had gone to Budapest he had decided that on his return he would look up his father and put to him all the questions that had so far never been uttered. There must, he had thought then, there must finally be an end to the silence. And during his stay in Budapest he had often thought so too, in fact on the train journey back to Vienna he had been busy the whole time working out different formulations – formulations, he said, with which he would at last be able to demand from his father the truth about his past.

But yesterday evening, he said – for some reason he hadn't thought of mentioning it to her – yesterday evening, as he said, he had bumped into him.

By pure coincidence.

"I had just arrived by train at Südbahnhof," he said, "and sat right at the back of the tram on the way in to the centre, when I suddenly to my great surprise saw him board the tram through the front entrance.

"I really hadn't expected to meet him so soon, I was convinced he was out at Nussdorf."

His father, on the other hand, he said, hadn't seen him.

"Father sat down on one of the benches right at the front, he took his hat off and was lost in thought. When the conductor came he gave a start, and when he dug out some money for his ticket his face assumed a confused, almost frightened expression which I had never seen on him before – and all at once it struck me how much he had aged recently.

"Father," he said, "suddenly seemed to me so unbearably old sitting there: huddled up, tired and wretched. His neck which stuck up out of his collar band seemed thin and bird-like, his head trembled slightly, his hair had grown almost white – and for the first time in my life I was seized not just by pity for him but in fact by something resembling tenderness.

"And then all at once I knew.

"Yes, at the very moment that I rose to go up to him I knew that I wouldn't ask anything – that not one of all the questions I had thought out would ever be asked.

"Why?" he said.

"Yes, now I ask myself why.

"From cowardice?

"From resignation – a feeling that it wouldn't serve any purpose anyway?

"Or because of something else that I can't see myself?"

His father, he continued, "had looked horrified when he caught sight of him. But when he had greeted him in a friendly fashion, he'd brightened up and asked him to sit down and tell him how his journey had gone. Father had explained that he had only been in town on a short errand and that in about an hour would already be returning to Nussdorf.

"Soon after that," he said, "he alighted at Schwarzenbergplatz.

"In the doorway he turned and declared that I was welcome out there at the weekend. I asked him to give Aunt my regards and promised to think about it.

"I myself", he said, "went on to Hockegasse".

Once again he lost the thread.

She waited.

"Magda…" he then said hesitantly.

"Magda," he whispered, "dearest…"

He looked out of the window.

Everything was silent and very still.

Then something happened.

It seemed to her as if she was suddenly being lifted by invisible hands.

As if by forces stronger than herself, she was being carried across the floor over to him.

Almost unwittingly she touched his arm slightly with her hand.

She felt him freeze.

But he didn't turn round to look at her, she realized that he didn't dare. She realized that he was afraid that he would frighten her away.

Afraid that he was mistaken.

While they both seemed to be waiting breathlessly for what was to happen the sun glided out from the clouds outside. The window became a looking-glass – yes, there they hovered, close to each other, light and translucent like shadows in the foliage of the trees.

He looked at her.

Their eyes met in the glass – and she smiled.